' . s| .... tale of everyday bleakness and
tr- .gression set in the seedy underworld of Paris. You
can smell the Gitanes and pastis fumes of the real France'
Maxim Jakubowski, *Guardian*

'Manotti effortlessly handles a fiendishly complicated plot.
Her characters are fully rounded and believable. And she is
funny, accurately reflecting the gallows humour that people
who frequently encounter horror often resort to as a defence'
Daily Telegraph

'A marvellously sophisticated, strong thriller … an
unflinching, knowledgeable and tough book … and a perfect
crime novel' Maxine, *Petrona*

'Truly labyrinthine skullduggery and a furious pace' *Kirkus
Reviews*

'Gets under the skin in a way that has rarely been so
compelling, and certainly never sexier' *Tribune*

'Manotti has Ellroy's gift for complex plotting, but she has
a grip on the economics, politics and social history which
marks her as special … good generic crime fiction, with *le
flair* in abundance' *TLS*

'Another excellent French crime writer to set alongside Fred
Vargas' *Publishing News*

'The complexity and the uncompromising tone have drawn
comparisons with American writers such as James Ellroy.
But Manotti's ability to convey the unique rhythms of a
French police investigation distinguishes *Rough Trade*'
Daily Telegraph

'Tightly written, undoubtedly realistic … exciting' *The Times*

D1079847

ESCAPE

DOMINIQUE MANOTTI

ESCAPE

Translated by Amanda Hopkinson and Ros Schwartz

ARCADIA BOOKS

Arcadia Books Ltd
139 Highlever Road
London W10 6PH

www.arcadiabooks.co.uk

First published in France as *L'Evasion* by Éditions Gallimard 2013
First published in the United Kingdom by Arcadia Books 2014

Copyright © Dominique Manotti 2013
Translation copyright © Amanda Hopkinson and Ros Schwartz 2014

A catalogue record for this book is available from the British Library.

ISBN 978-1-909807-55-6

Typeset in Minion by MacGuru Ltd
Printed and bound by CPI Group (UK) Ltd., Croydon CRO 4YY

This book is supported by the Institut Français (Royaume-
Uni) as part of the Burgess programme. Arcadia Books
would like to thank them for their generous support.

Arcadia Books supports English PEN *www.englishpen.org* and
The Book Trade Charity *http://www.btbs.org*

Arcadia Books distributors are as follows:

in the UK and elsewhere in Europe:
Macmillan Distribution Ltd
Brunel Road

ESCAPE

CHAPTER ONE

FEBRUARY–MARCH 1987

8 February, near Rome
The bins stink. A huge skip with black plastic rubbish bags spilling on to the concrete floor, a poky little room with no windows lit by two flickering fluorescent tubes, blocked off by a metal shutter and an iron gate. Filippo is furious. Usually, when he comes to sweep out and clean the bin room, the rubbish trucks have already been, the skips are empty and the stench is not too bad. But today the smell is almost unbearable. He sets to work, gagging. He sweeps and scrubs the floor, then sloshes bleach and buckets of water over it. Six months inside, another 410 days to go, desperate to get out, but how? Then what? He hurls a final bucket of water and glances at his watch. In a quarter of an hour, his shift will be over. Time to clock out, go back up to his cell ... *410 days, fuck, another 410 days* ... Suddenly, the motor controlling the metal shutter from the outside starts up and the shutter begins to vibrate. Panic. This has never happened before. He isn't supposed to be there when the gate opens. *What do I do?* Terrified, he glances at his watch. *No, this is when I should be here.* A dull thudding sound comes from the rubbish chute, something banging against the walls, and a curled-up body catapults headlong into the skip then unfurls and dives into the refuse. Filippo just has time to recognise his cellmate, Carlo. A stream of incoherent reactions, *My only friend breaking out ... and without me ...* The metal shutter begins to rise, letting in a shaft of sunlight across the floor. *I'm here when he breaks out, I'll be accused of aiding*

and abetting him and I'll get another year at least … in solitary.
Without a second thought, Filippo jumps, arms raised, grabs
the top of the skip, steadies himself with acrobatic agility and
plunges into the mound of refuse. He hears Carlo swear under
his breath and say, 'For fuck's sake bury yourself and cover
your face,' and then loses contact. He pulls his T-shirt up over
his face, closes his eyes and swims down between the bags
towards the bottom of the skip. The plastic is nice and slip-
pery, but the smell and the weight are suffocating. A torn bag
and his head and arms are covered in sticky, viscous, rotting,
scratchy matter. And that stink. He vomits. All over his face.
*Calm down, stop panicking, otherwise I'm dead. Get this T-shirt
off, wipe my face, breathe calmly, short breaths, protect my
nose and mouth.* His body curls into a ball, Filippo tries to
open up an air-pocket by extending his arms very slowly. He
listens to the sounds coming from outside. The truck has just
dropped off an empty skip. He pictures the guards positioned
all around the yard. Now the truck is about to load their skip.
Its sides clanging, the skip rises through the air as it is winched
up, one more thud and it is on the truck. A pause, the operators must be attaching the tarpaulin … engine starting up,
they are on the move, a pause, his heart now thumping, the
guards must be lifting up the tarpaulin, inspecting the skip's
contents. Filippo huddles tighter, the truck is off again, at a
steady speed. He is out. Incredulity. *What on earth am I doing
here?* He briefly loses consciousness.

The skip is swiftly emptied. Their bodies are thrown out
and they roll among the bags and the refuse. Already on his
feet, Carlo grabs the semi-conscious Filippo's arm and forces
him to get up. They are standing thigh-deep in a mountain
of rubbish. Dazed, Filippo looks around him and notices an
industrial building and a brick factory-chimney on his right,
and on his left a very high, very smooth wall against which
the refuse is tipped. *Is this the taste, the smell of freedom? Not
really.* Carlo doesn't give him time to collect himself, he pulls,

pushes and shoves him, forcing him to run down the mound of rubbish, then drags him towards the perimeter wall. In front of him stands a ladder. 'Up!' commands Carlo, thumping him in the back, 'Get a move on.' Filippo climbs the ladder in a daze, swings over the wall and tumbles down the other side. Carlo jumps down nimbly just behind him and helps him up. A car awaits them, engine running, doors open, and they fling themselves on to the rear seat. The smell is unbearable. The driver – wearing dark glasses, his coat collar turned up to conceal the lower part of his face – opens the windows and pulls away at speed. Seated next to him a girl, head held stiffly, face covered by a headscarf. Without turning around, she says:

'So who's this?'

Filippo hears Carlo's tense voice:

'Drive, drive, we'll talk when we can stop.'

They are lying side by side on the floor in the back of the car. Bumps and bends, they must be driving fast along a country road. Filippo feels all his muscles contract and ache. He makes himself breathe, protects his head and let his mind go blank.

The car comes to an abrupt stop, the engine switches off, the door opens. Carlo taps Filippo on the shoulder, making him start, and points to a clump of trees about a hundred metres away.

'Wait for me over there, I won't be a minute.'

Filippo straightens up, takes a few steps, stiff at first, aching, confused, then he freezes, completely overwhelmed, stunned by the sight that greets him. He is standing beside a tumble-down dry-stone barn on a shelf jutting out from the mountain-side. Down below lies a blue-green lake, and opposite him a white, rocky ridge, vivid against a vast blue sky. He feels giddy. He opens his arms wide and breathes deeply. The air is very pure, sharp. He feels it enter his lungs and cleanse the stench of the bins and the vomit. *The calm, the silence, the beauty,* that is the word that sums it up for him. A surprising word for a kid from a working-class district of Rome who's never admired a landscape. He sets off again, walking slowly, swaying slightly, shivering with cold, surprised to be in one piece, at liberty, and in the middle of the mountains.

Without thinking, he turns round, perhaps to speak to Carlo, or to seek reassurance that he is there and will be joining him. Carlo is there, his back to him. Standing before him is the girl from the car, not very tall, her perfect oval face raised towards him in the full sunlight. She is talking to him earnestly, perhaps angrily. Her headscarf has slid down on to her shoulders freeing a mass of fair hair that glints copper-coloured in the sun, ruffled by the wind. The image etches itself on his memory. The girl with coppery lights in her hair and the mountains, the beauty of freedom. Carlo puts his arms around her, leans slowly towards her mouth and kisses her in a lengthy embrace. Behind them stands the driver who has turned down his coat collar, removed his dark glasses and is staring at the couple formed by Carlo and the girl. Filippo is struck by the man's appearance – a square jaw, deep-set eyes beneath very dark eyebrows that form a thick, continuous line across his face, and a scar on his left cheek that drags his eyelid downwards. The overall effect is thuggish. When the driver notices that Filippo is watching the three of them, he suddenly looks furious and raises his hand. Scared, Filippo quickly turns round without waiting to see how the gesture finishes, and walks towards the clump of trees as instructed by Carlo, with a sense of having committed a serious offence, but not knowing what. In such situations, his strategy has always been to take refuge in deepest silence and switch off his mind, without attempting to understand.

He sits down with his back to the trees, staring out over the valley, and lets himself be entranced by the landscape.

Carlo comes over, hands him a pullover that he puts on straight away, and crouches down beside him.

'We hadn't expected you to be in the bin room…'

'I had no choice. I'm always there at that time. The truck was late, it arrived while I was cleaning. I was surprised, because it's never happened before.'

'…and certainly not that you would jump into the skip.'

'I didn't think. I saw you and just followed.'

'What are you going to do now?'

'Stay with you. Can't I?'

'No.'

'Then I have no idea.'

'We part company here.' He places a canvas bag at Filippo's feet. 'I've put everything I could find in the cars in there for you. Clothes, two sandwiches, and some money.' Carlo pauses, Filippo says nothing. 'My escape will be in the news, I think. And they'll be looking for you, because you broke out with me. You'll have to keep a low profile for a while, until things settle down.' A pause, Filippo still saying nothing. 'Do you understand what I'm telling you?'

A nod. Filippo continues to gaze at the mountains.

'If things get too tough here in Italy, go over to France. Here, on this envelope, I've written the address of Lisa Biaggi, in Paris. Go there and say I sent you, tell her what happened. She'll help you.' Filippo takes the envelope without looking at Carlo and slips it in the bag. Carlo stands up.

'Goodbye, Filippo. Take care of yourself.'

And he leaves, walking fast and without turning round.

A little later Filippo hears the sound of an engine coming from behind the ruined barn. He sits rigid for what feels like ages. Then he sees a car driving alongside the lake, down below. It looks tiny, out of place in this wilderness. Carlo is inside, for sure. The car disappears behind the rocky ridge. Agony. The sun is setting behind Filippo and the rock face opposite turns pink, then grey. It is dark. Filippo is exhausted. He feels bereft, lost, helpless. Orphaned. Unable to pursue a coherent train of thought, he simply lets time flow past. When he starts to shiver with cold, he gets up, returns to the dilapidated barn and finds the car that brought them there, hidden under a half-collapsed roof. He lifts the bonnet – the spark plugs have been removed and wires ripped out. He slides under the rear seat, wraps himself in a blanket lying on the floor and falls asleep, his head resting on the canvas bag.

When he wakens, the sun has just risen behind the white rocks. The light is sharp, pitiless. Filippo changes into clean clothes. He feels relaxed. He goes out and sits facing the sun, slowly eating a sandwich and drinking some fresh water. *Where the hell am I? Lost. Jumping into that skip was a bad move. Serves me right. I thought that my cellmate – working-class and proud of it, a political prisoner, educated, a smooth talker and avid reader – was my friend, a friend to the street kid who can barely read, incapable of stringing together three sentences. Idiot. In your dreams. Dumped like a girl.* Bitterness and resentment. *OK, so I don't know where I am, but do I know where I'm going?* A vision of the car, the previous evening, driving away along the lakeshore. *I know where I'm heading, the exit's that way. Then what? Rome? My family? I've slammed the door, I'm not going home a loser. And the cops will get there before me. Go back to my Termini station gang, back to fleecing tourists and selling contraband cigarettes? Endlessly fighting over cash, a girl, a carton of fags, the cops who'll pay off anyone willing to snitch on their mates, sit next to the guy who might have been the one who grassed on me and shake his hand. The filth, the violence, permanently stoned. I've had enough. When I was inside, I dreamed of something different.*

They used to sit side by side on the narrow lower bunk, passing a joint back and forth cupped in their palms, and Carlo would talk nonstop, very quietly in the dark, occasionally punctuated by desperate howls, muffled thumping on the walls, the screws on their rounds. He recounted his memories to Filippo, at first grim, of going to work in the Milan factories as a very young man, bewildered by the brutality of a factory worker's life. Then, very soon, the workers' protests of the late sixties began. Carlo told him about the meetings in his workshop, in his factory, which soon became a daily event. Each person took the floor, and each person's view was given equal weight. There was an initial forging of collective thinking and a collective will. Carlo would grow excited as he recalled the euphoria of discovering the strength of men acting in unison, all equal, of workers' marches through the factory that started spontaneously after the meetings, going from workshop to workshop, discovering a world that, until then, had been mysterious and threatening, where the men were not permitted to move around freely. In a great burst of elation, solidarity and hope, they had believed that the factory belonged to them, that it had become their territory. He and his comrades, along with so many others, had tied red scarves around their necks to demonstrate their pride and their determination. They had driven out the hated bosses, had begun to reorganise their workload and the production process. Carlo still talked about the outbursts of wild joy, like that night in Milan when he and his friends set fire to all the bosses' cars at the same time. It made for an enthralling fireworks display and was a way of taking power over the city, a sacred revenge. It hadn't lasted long, but to experience that, at least once in a lifetime ... Filippo listened, rapt. He felt every word resonate in his body. The factory had never been what he wanted, working as slave labour, for so little return. But the tightly knit group, standing together for better or for worse, collective struggle and violence as a way of life, the hope of overturning everything one day – that was something he had always dreamed of. Among Rome's street gangs, he had never found more than a distant, distorted echo of his dreams and his desperation, the battle for survival of all against all, without ever having the words to express it.

Today he could see it all very clearly; he envied Carlo and the Milan workers.

Carlo went on, 'The old world was fracturing, it was the dawn of a new era, but we couldn't find the right words to describe the world we were in the process of inventing, and to carry an entire people along with us. We spoke a turgid, out-dated language, one we had inherited, the language of the old world that we wanted to bury. Naturally, no one understood us, any better than I think we did ourselves. If only there'd been a modern Victor Hugo in our factories to tell our story, just think … our fate might have been different. Who knows? There are moments like that when worlds can be turned upside down.' And on that note he fell silent, absorbed in his memories and his dreams. Filippo, sitting beside him in the dark, feeling the warmth of his body, carried on listening to his silences, moved to tears, without trying to understand why. Victor Hugo, no, he couldn't think like that. He didn't know who Hugo was, but he told himself that one day, perhaps, he would.

Carlo resumed, on a more sombre, despairing note, 'History very soon abandoned us, we'd probably got it all wrong, prob-ably realised too late. The bosses reshaped the economic order. A globalised market – that was the watchword. It felt as though the factory, our world, the only world we knew, the focus of all our struggles, our pride and even our lives, was slipping through our fingers. Plants were relocated, we didn't know where, the machinery changed, and with it, the way pro-duction was organised. Power was vested in the white-collar workers, the teams of shop-floor workers were broken up, we felt the need to expand the battlefield, come out of the factory so we weren't suffocated to death inside. In December '69, the henchmen of the neo-fascists, the Italian secret service and the CIA, exploded a bomb in a Milan bank, Piazza Fontana. It left seventeen dead, dozens injured. Do you remember, Filippo?'

'Vaguely. I wasn't really interested. Milan was a long way north.'

'After that, there were more bomb explosions. Brescia, the *Italicus* train. The Italian secret service was murdering its own people. They were using chaos and terror to fight us, to rebuild a major anti-Communist, anti-red front. Whenever we demonstrated, there were tens of thousands of us in the streets. We thought we were the people. We believed we were strong enough to follow them and fight them on the battleground they'd chosen, outside the factory, weapons in hand. And besides, we were the sons of the 1917 Russian revolution, of the Turin workers' councils, of the Italian Communist Party and of the Italian Resistance. Memories of violent struggle were still so vivid, so close, in our families and in the factories.'

After a lengthy hesitation, Carlo said, 'I'm going to tell you a childhood memory.' Filippo was surprised, childhood memories were not part of Carlo's usual repertoire, but he waited, in silence. 'When I was a kid, I used to spend my holidays with my grandparents, farmers in the Bologna region. Once a year, on the 5th of August, always on the same date, probably some anniversary, my grandfather would take me down to the bottom of the vegetable garden, behind a hedge. We'd dig up a metal case and he'd open it. It contained two guns wrapped in rags. Each year, he would say solemnly, "Walther P38 pistols, captured from the Germans." He'd take them apart on a blanket, oil them very carefully, making me touch the metal and inhale the smell of oil, then he'd reassemble them and pack them away, and we'd bury the case again, always in the same place. "So there's no risk of making a mistake when we need to dig them up. Sometimes you have to act fast," he'd say. "They're my weapons from when I was in the Resistance. You never know." When I went to look for them years later, my grandfather already long since dead, I couldn't find them.' Carlo had a lump in his throat. He was silent for a while. Then he continued in a hoarse voice. 'So we took up arms. We risked our lives, we risked death each day, but that's not what is so terrible, the terrible thing is killing. And we killed. I killed. And our fathers cursed us.' There followed a long silence. In Carlo's life, the intensity of conviction and the violence of hope had swept everything away, smashed everything. And Filippo contemplated the wreckage, fascinated.

Then Carlo would say, 'Those were different times. My grandfather never knew about all that. Just as well. I couldn't have stood it if he'd cursed me. Go to sleep, Filippo, we'll still be here tomorrow and we can carry on talking.' And Filippo would clamber into the top bunk and fall asleep, happy, his head full of confused dreams.

I listened, every night for six months. Thinking it over now, alone in the mountains, abandoned and betrayed, it just sounds weird.

Forget all that, otherwise I'm stuffed.

Filippo gets up, stretches, grabs the bag, slings it over his shoulder and begins the descent towards the lake. His mind is made up. It will be Milan.

10 February, Paris

Lisa Biaggi leads a well-ordered life. Every morning she leaves her little apartment in Rue de Belleville early, takes the Métro from Belleville and commutes to La Défense where she works as a medical secretary in an occupational health centre. On the way to l'Étoile, she stops to buy the previous day's Italian newspapers from a kiosk that stocks a good range of international papers for the tourists. She doesn't open them straight away but lingers for a moment, her mind free. Today it is sunny and bright, like a promise of spring. She sits on a café terrace at the top of the Champs-Élysées, the sun shining on her face, and orders a cappuccino and croissants. This is the best part of the day, and she relishes it. She has been a political refugee in France since 1980 and has found a steady job that enables her to live in relative comfort, but somehow she still cannot resign herself to making her life here. She has turned forty. She can feel her body, her face, and her mind wither as she waits to return, but there is nothing to be done, and each day the news from home reawakens the ache of exile. She contemplates the swelling crowds walking past and sighs. Her cappuccino drunk, nearly time to resume her commute, and she opens the *Corriere della Sera* and begins to flick through it. A shock. On the inside pages, a photo of Carlo. Carlo, her man, the love of her life. Headline: Spectacular jailbreak … Her heart thumping, blurred vision, her eyes jump from one line to the next.

In a refuse truck … with his cellmate, Filippo Zuliani, a small-time crook … accomplices among the truck drivers. The police are actively looking for the two fugitives … Photos of the two men. The small-time crook has the mug of a small-time crook. What the hell was Carlo doing with him? It is worrying.

She folds the newspaper and tries to convince herself that Carlo will be all right, that he isn't dead, but it is no good, she can visualise him dead. She picks up her belongings and heads for the Métro, towards La Défense and her office. It is too soon or too late to cry.

At La Vielleuse, Rue de Belleville, Lisa is playing pool, seemingly absorbed in the game, her long, slim form leaning over the baize, her face masked by her shoulder-length black hair, her movements precise. A habit that goes back more than eight years, to the time of her first clandestine missions in Paris, when Carlo was the main contact for the organisation back in Milan. Playing pool occupies both hands and mind when you're waiting for a phone call, night after night, at a set time. Lisa has come to enjoy the game, and she has carried on playing since Carlo's arrest, even though there is no longer anything to wait for. She is even considered to be a good player by the little group of regulars who are very respectful of her. You don't often find a woman who plays well. But today, as in the old days, she is playing to kill time. Carlo is free again … the old underground habits, why not? The phone rings for the third time that evening. Each time she jumps, just as before. The owner picks up the phone, looks over and signals to her, this time it is for her. She dashes over to the old phone booth, closed off, discreet, right at the back of the room, as before.

'Lisa, it's me.'

Despite the overwhelming emotion, hearing his voice live for the first time in seven years makes her want to laugh. Who else could it be? A telephone date that has been on hold for seven years...

'I know.'

'I knew I'd find you. I love you.'

'I'm frightened, Carlo.'

'Everything's OK. I don't have much time. Listen carefully. The leadership of our organisation has declared that they're laying down their arms, they've admitted defeat.'

'I know, I still read the papers.'

'They're doing the right thing, I agree, even though I would like to have been consulted. But this changes things. I continued the struggle for seven years in jail, without letting up, I carried out all my instructions. But now we're laying down our arms, it makes no sense to stay banged up. I have no liking for long, drawn-out, tragic deaths.'

'So?'

'So I'm leaving.'

'Just like that?'

'Yes, just like that. You remember? We used to call that "practising the objective". When we consider a demand to be right and necessary, we enact it, we don't wait for it to be handed to us. I've seized my freedom.'

'That's crazy, now the Red Brigades are announcing they're laying down their arms, you'll be released within a few months. And perhaps the rest of us will be able to come back home.'

'Never. You're talking as if you don't know how the government works. They hate us because we exposed their rotten schemes and we frightened them, really frightened them. They found out that perhaps they were mortal. Now that they've won, they're going to make us pay for it, they're taking their revenge and will continue to do so, there'll never be an amnesty, they'll let us rot in jail or in exile until the end of time...'

'It's not possible, Carlo, there are still some democrats in Italy...'

'Don't be naive. Are you aware of how many emergency laws they've introduced, how many of our people are in jail? Five thousand? More? You've seen the new law on dissociation? First the *penitenti,* those turned informants, then those who've formally repented. Just you wait, there'll be havoc, we're going to wither on the vine. Everything will fall apart, they'll do their utmost to wipe us out, one by one. Our politicians, pseudo-democrats included, are pathetic, incompetent and vindictive.'

'Maybe. But does that improve your chances of survival?'

'At least I'll have tried. I don't want to give them the satisfaction of seeing me die in jail. I do not repent, I do not dissociate myself from the movement, I renounce nothing, and I'm appalled by those who do, but fuck them, fuck those who've won. I'll get hold of some money and an ID – taking as few risks as possible – and I'm out of here. I'll go and live abroad, in the open.'

'I've been worried ever since they transferred you to that prison for common criminals, six months ago. I thought there was something odd about that. I'm afraid of a trap. And now your cellmate...'

'Don't be paranoid, Lisa.'

'Am I naive or am I para?'

'Both. Don't worry. My cellmate and I have already parted company.'

'What about the accomplices they mention in the papers?'

'The truck drivers. They're not politicos, but small-time crooks. They were paid, they're protected and they know nothing. My two current companions aren't politicos either and I'm certain of them. Lisa, give me time to find the money and get my ID sorted, it's all been planned, organised, it won't be hard, I won't put myself in danger, and then I'll go abroad. I'll call you and you can come and join me. My next call will be the beginning of our new life. I love you, Lisa...'

'Stop. Be quiet. It's too painful. I'll wait for your next call.'

She hangs up. Her feelings of anguish are still just as sharp. The truck drivers aren't politicos, does that make them reliable? *No risks*, she doesn't believe that. Death lurks. She leans against the glass side of the booth and gets her breath back. Then resumes the game of pool.

February–March, central Italy, in the mountains

Filippo is heading in a north-north-easterly direction. It is a glorious day, with a bright, late-winter sun. He walks at dawn, the coldest time of day, to warm up, and takes a siesta in the hot midday sun, washing sometimes, not often, in the freezing rivers, and sheltering at night in ruins, in the bushes, to grab as much sleep as he can. He makes his way over the mountains, not moving too far away from the plain, stopping in villages to buy bread and cheese. He covers a good twenty kilometres a day. The paths are steep, the going tough, especially since he has never practised any sport beyond sprinting frantically through the streets of Rome to shake off the cops, but he finds it surprisingly enjoyable. After the noisy life he has lived these past years, first in Rome's squats, then in jail, he is discovering the tranquillity of the low mountain area and gradually becoming used to it, seeing it as a protective cocoon, listening to what his body is telling him. His muscles are becoming trim and toned, and he inhales the mountain air deeply. He listens to the words, the sentences that form in his head with no shape or purpose, and rejoices in his freedom, with no ties and no future.

One day, after walking for over a week, he rounds a bend and comes to the point where the mountains meet the plain. Spread bright in the sunshine, like a toy within his grasp, is the austere shape of a city built entirely of stone, a jungle of towers surrounded by walls, a stone universe in tones of yellow and white. From this distance, there are no visible signs of human life. There is something very familiar about this city. He has already seen it, or its twin, in a big, framed photo on the wall behind the till of the Guidoriccio da Fogliano bistro, where his mother regularly sent him to fetch his father when he was too drunk to find his own way home. In the photo, stone cities form the backdrop to a conqueror in armour and a silk tunic, sitting bolt upright on his horse, alone, the only living being in a landscape of white rocks studded with fortifications and spears. He is silhouetted against a black sky, at war with the entire earth and all its gods, aware that he is posing for eternity. Solitude is his kingdom. That conqueror of wildernesses and empty cities has been the hero of his daydreams ever since he was a child in search of his identity. He fervently admired the magnificent figure, both victorious warrior and exterminating angel who destroys all forms of life in his path. When he imagined himself at the warrior's side, he felt a mixture of fear and desire that gave him a delicious thrill. These are the best of his childhood memories.

Memories come flooding back to haunt him as he makes his way across the godforsaken landscape in his improbable bid for escape. Even if today the agony of those empty cities overwhelms the glory of the conqueror – merely a matter of viewpoint – the familiar image is a comfort to Filippo, giving him the strange reassurance that he is not utterly lost. He hails the town in the distance and continues on his way.

4 March, Bologna

Filippo walks on. The days flow into one another, without distinction, all exactly the same. He has lost count of time.

Two or three weeks later, he comes to a huge church standing on a ridge, secluded among the trees. He ventures as far as the square in front of it. Ahead of him the steep mountainside drops down on to a plain that stretches as far as the horizon. At his feet, not far away, lies Bologna with its towers and belfries, its heart of brown stone and pink-tiled roofs ringed by modern neighbourhoods, teeming with life. The hubbub of the city rises up and reaches his ears. He stops in his tracks. He has trekked all the way to the north. A bitter memory of the rejection that had landed him right here, where he stands, on a crest between two worlds. The certainty that he is lost. Fear. *You'll have to keep a low profile for a while, until things settle down.* How will he know when things have settled down? Hide, forever? In front of the church a path leads straight out of the porch and down into the city in one straight line. Partly a path, partly steps, its many yellow-and-red luminous arches trumpet the joy of returning to the company of humans, the bustle of the streets, people jostling, bumping into one another, conversing perhaps. Surprises, discoveries, woes, the thousand snippets of urban life in constant flux, the end of solitude and within reach, a few hundred metres away, the temptation is too strong. Filippo launches himself downhill, and without a second thought begins to run, racing down the steep incline, jumping from step to step, caution to the winds.

After visiting the public baths, a hairdresser and a barber, Filippo buys the newspaper and sits on a café terrace to flick through it over an espresso. Not that he is used to going to the barber's or reading the newspaper, but these seem to be appropriate rituals to mark his return to city life. He unfolds the newspaper and glances at it distractedly, when a headline catches his eye.

IS RED TERRORISM MAKING A GRAND COMEBACK?
Former Red Brigades leader killed in failed bank heist in Milan.

Friends of Carlo's, maybe? The introductory paragraph leaps out at him:

Red Brigades veteran Carlo Fedeli, who escaped from of prison three weeks ago, was shot dead yesterday outside the Piemonte-Sardegna bank at 10 Via Del Battifolle, Milan during an attempted raid...

His vision blurred by tears, he sits doubled up, breathless. His sense of rejection, of betrayal by Carlo is so powerful that he has completely erased all memory of him. It returns with a vengeance. *'You'll have to keep a low profile ... Take care of yourself.' You didn't forsake me, you went to war, and you were trying to protect me. But I thought you were ditching me, I didn't trust you, I'm the one who's a traitor. I'm ashamed of myself.* When he regains his breath, he continues reading.

Yesterday, Friday 3 March, at around 3 p.m., Via Del Battifolle in Milan, a security van drew up outside the Piemonte-Sardegna bank. Two armed security guards, Massimo Gasparini and Fredo Albrizio, alighted and entered the bank, where they were scheduled to spend no more than two minutes. They are professionals. The times of their stop-offs change every day as a precaution, but on this occasion, they were anticipated. As they entered the bank, two vans positioned themselves on the driveway entrances on either side of the façade, blocking the section of pavement outside the bank from view. The two guards emerged, one carrying two bags, the other with his hand on his holster. Carlo Fedeli leapt out of the right-hand van, brandishing a gun, and yelled at the armed guard to put his hands up, while his two accomplices burst out of the other van and snatched the bags. At that moment, by the most extraordinary coincidence, two *carabinieri* came out of the bank, where one of them, a regular customer at the branch, had just paid in some cheques. Everything happened very fast. The two *carabinieri* went for their guns. Carlo Fedeli turned towards them, aiming his gun. A shot rang out, perhaps fired by one of the security guards or by Fedeli's accomplices. Fearing for his life, Brigadier Lucio Renzi then fired, killing Carlo Fedeli outright. Realising that the operation had failed, Fedeli's two accomplices fled, covering themselves with a burst of gunfire and killing one of the *carabinieri*, Giorgio Barbieri, aged twenty-eight, married, father of two children aged three and one, as well as one of the security guards – Nino Gasparini, also married and father of a five-year-old little girl. Then they made off, probably using one or two motorbikes for their getaway. Both vans were stolen. They are being examined by the forensics team, so far yielding no results.

The police have not yet identified the fugitives, but they have a reliable lead.

Supposing it isn't true? A stupid reaction. Filippo adopts an air of indifference, rises and goes to buy two other papers from the nearby kiosk. He returns to his table and opens out the papers. The same story is there in black and white. In one of the papers, there is even a double-page spread with a photo showing the three bodies covered with tarpaulins, pools of blood on the pavement. So it is true. No getting away from it. Now he can wallow in his misery, his eyes glued to the photo. A few tears. Memories. The long conversations, friendship, admiration even, for that man who was such a good talker. *From listening to him all the time, I ended up thinking that the story he was telling was my story too, in a way. I feel gutted, it's like a big hole in my life.* Then, like an electric shock, Carlo's words suddenly come back to him with clarity: *'My escape will be in the news, I think. And they'll be looking for you, because you broke out with me. You'll have to keep a low profile for a while, until things settle down.'* There had been a long silence, and then Carlo had said, 'Do you understand what I'm saying?' Of course not, at that point, he didn't understand, and now he feels guilty. Those words weigh heavily on him. *'My escape will be in the news.'* Why *'his'* escape? *It was mine too, wasn't it? I must find papers that talk about 'our' escape, that's vital. Where can I get hold of them?* Filippo folds his newspapers, puts them in his bag, pays for his coffee, and sets off in search of the public library.

At the library, the entire national daily press from the past month is available free of charge, and there is hardly anyone around. Filippo quickly finds the papers from the week of their breakout, but he is in too much of an emotional state to remember the exact date. He takes the papers from the entire week and sits down at an isolated desk, his back to the public.

Almost immediately, he comes across the headline in *La Stampa*, 'Former Red Brigades Leader Escapes.' Below it, two photos, Carlo's, and his own. Another electric shock. A photo of him, Filippo, on the front page of the newspaper. It makes no sense. He closes his eyes, runs his hands over the photo, looks at it again – it is still there, he'll have to face it. He reads the caption, 'Filippo Zuliani, common prisoner and Carlo Fedeli's cellmate, key accomplice in a meticulously planned jailbreak.'

Accomplice in a meticulously planned jailbreak. This time, he feels sheer panic. The police are looking for the accomplices to the bank robbery, the cop killers, and they have a reliable lead. *I am the reliable lead. A key accomplice in a meticulously planned jailbreak and unable to prove that I was walking alone in the mountains at the time of the bank robbery. Unable to prove that I wasn't on the pavement outside that bank in Milan, where I've never set foot in my life. In a way, his story is my story. No, it's not just partly my story, but one I'm in up to my neck. If the cops get their hands on me, I'm fucked. And my photo, right here in the paper.* He runs his hand over his face. *That was stupid, going to the barber's. How come no one's recognised me yet?* An insane urge to run away. *Resist it. Keep a low profile. Must put the newspapers back.* Breaking out into an anxious sweat, his hands clammy, his back rigid, he walks over and puts the newspapers back on the shelves, checks that they are in precisely the right order, and makes his way to the exit. Nothing happens. He leaves. No one tries to stop him.

He wanders aimlessly through the streets, sits down on a bench and tries to muster his thoughts. *Two dead. They're going to pin two deaths on me. Two deaths including a* carabiniere. *Not me, not two deaths, it makes no sense. I'll never last out. I'm not made of that stuff. Only one solution, run, vanish. 'If things get too tough here in Italy, go over to France. Here, on this envelope, Lisa Biaggi, in Paris. Say I sent you and tell her what happened. She'll help you.'* He'd forgotten all about her. He thrusts his hand in the bag and rummages around feverishly. The envelope with Lisa's address is there, right at the bottom. Salvation.

CHAPTER TWO

MARCH 1987, PARIS

5 March

Since learning of Carlo's death from the papers, Lisa has shut herself up in her studio apartment. It is on the fourth floor of an ancient building in Rue de Belleville, at the far end of an overgrown courtyard garden. She sits there for hours in a state of shock, huddled in an armchair in front of the tall window of her living area, looking out over the trees. Overcome by grief she nibbles, drinks coffee, thinks, sleeps and gets up from the chair as little as possible.

It all began in the autumn of '69 when she was a young rookie journalist at *L'Unità*, daily newspaper of the Italian Communist Party, then at the height of its powers. She was sent to Milan to report live from the Siemens factory where 'something was happening'. She still feels emotional when she remembers her awe (the word is no exaggeration) on discovering the factory in ferment. At that time, people called it 'in a state of revolution', and for her and a few thousand people, that word meant something. She fell out with *L'Unità*, which rejected her articles and cut off her source of income, and met one of the workers, Carlo, a good-looker and a smooth talker. It was love, naturally. Had she fallen in love with him, or with that moment when young workers believed they were making history? The question made no sense, it was simply their life. She had followed Carlo into the Red Brigades. Years later Lisa was in France, sent by the organisation to meet a delegation of Palestinians. That was in 1980, and by then, hope had already died, and she was carrying on out of loyalty (to what? to whom? pointless questions? Loyalty to herself, to her past). While she was away, the police had surrounded their apartment in Milan, arrested Carlo and two other comrades and confiscated all their files. Carlo got a message to her via their lawyers that the police were actively looking for her, and that she should stay in France, at least for a while. At least for a while – and that had been seven years ago. Without seeing Carlo again, and without admitting to herself that the separation was permanent. Well now it is. Now he has been assassinated.

If I were a journalist, in Italy, in my real life ... I'd investigate. The security guards change their route and their schedule every day. Who informed Carlo, who decided on the date and the place of the assassination? I'd want to know about the two *carabinieri*, that has to be the easiest starting point. Talk to the bank staff, they go for coffee in a nearby café in their lunch break, and they like to talk. Especially about sensational events of this kind, in which they have been directly involved. Yes, they would well remember the two *carabinieri* on that day; no, the men would not have paid in a cheque, and actually no, they would not recall ever seeing them before the day of the shooting.

I'd want to talk to *Carabiniere* Lucio Renzi. He is supposed to have come out of the bank and walked straight into an armed robbery, and killed Carlo with a single bullet in the chest. He is notorious for being trigger-happy. What is his career history? Between the infamous P2 Masonic Lodge veterans filled with resentment and the enemies of the P2 Lodge veterans, you can always get the information you need from the Italian police. And if Renzi had worked with the secret service for a while, it would all add up. This was no aborted bank robbery, it was an assassination.

Lisa stares out at the courtyard and the trees bending in the wind. The air is turning chilly. She closes the window. *But I'm not a journalist, I'm not in my real life, I'm here, in exile, in France. I left my entire life behind in Italy. I know who those*

people are over there. I know them, I understand them, I'm cut
from the same cloth, I know the networks. From here, I watch
that whole world growing restless, but I can't reach out to it. It's
as if I'm shut up in a glass cage. I stretch out my hand, I touch
the glass, but I can't get a grip on anything. I am an exile.

A few discreet taps at the door. Lisa hesitates, then opens it.
Roberto. He hugs her.

'I came as soon as I heard. As quickly as I could.'

She rests her head on his shoulder and cries silently, not for
long. No point in talking. They have too many shared memories – they both know what Carlo's death means. Then she
pulls away.

'Shall I make you a tea, or a coffee?'

'Coffee, please.'

She goes over to the kitchenette, splashes some water on
her face, and fills the cafetière. He sinks into one of the two
armchairs in the sitting-room area, without taking his eyes
off her. Her tall, erect, slightly stiff outline, immaculate grey
sweatshirt and trousers, her carefully brushed mass of black
hair, her smooth face, her eyes only slightly puffy – why does
she need to keep up appearances?

'You're coping … better than I am, I'd say…' She shrugs. 'Are
you coming to the meeting between the Italian refugees and
the lawyers tomorrow?'

'No.'

She sets two cups of coffee and a packet of dry biscuits down
on the coffee table, and seats herself in the other armchair.

'I don't want to have to listen to people I don't know very
well – people who didn't know or love Carlo – talking to me
about his death. I don't want to have to answer questions. But
I'm glad you're here, Roberto, because when I'm with you I feel
like talking, and it helps. I am carrying a huge burden. I felt
his death coming, I was living with it for the last six months,
without saying a word, not even to you…'

Roberto leans towards her, listening attentively.

'...ever since he was transferred to that prison for common criminals. He was set up, Roberto, his escape and his assassination were planned.'

'What makes you say that?'

'First of all, his transfer. No reason, other than that it's impossible to escape from high-security prisons. Then, the articles in the papers – they're all the same, as if they were publishing an official press release. And no mention of their source. Because that source is the same for all of them, it's the police. That ridiculous claim that the two *carabinieri* went to the bank to pay in some cheques, that one of them had an account there, that he was a regular customer. A bit over-the-top, don't you think? And no one went to sniff around, check the facts, interview witnesses. It's as if they're scared to touch it because it stinks.'

Roberto drinks his coffee, gingerly sets his cup down and frowns. He remains sceptical.

'Not convincing. Journalists nearly always work that way, regurgitating police sources without checking them. What else?'

'The small-time crook who broke out with him. Does that sound like Carlo, teaming up with a common criminal?'

'He spent seven years inside, Lisa. That changes a man.'

'What about the two *carabinieri* who "happened" to be coming out of the bank at that precise moment. I don't buy that.'

'Who would have engineered the whole show? The people who helped him escape? With three dead, that's a bit much, don't you think? But more importantly, why?'

'To kill the declaration that the original Red Brigades leaders have just published.'

'That's a bit of a sledgehammer to crack a nut, isn't it?'

'The stakes are high for us, Roberto. Don't underestimate them. That open letter could be the starting point for a collective analysis. We need to read it and discuss it, together and with other left-wing organisations. So we need time, and we need calm. If we don't analyse our defeat, each of us will be left to our own individual solitude and despair. Our generation will be airbrushed out, our history will be erased, and the traitors and scumbags will triumph.'

'Nobody wants that debate, neither the left – or what remains of it – nor the right. Definitely not with us. We're terrorists, outcasts.'

'Exactly. A few days after the publication of the Red Brigades' open letter, one of their former leaders raids a bank and kills a *carabiniere*. On the front page of all the papers, "Red terrorism from left-wing extremists, still a threat, is now pure gangsterism. Why should we open a dialogue with these people?" Don't you find it too much of a coincidence that this sabotages all our chances of entering into a political dialogue?'

'Carlo could very well have lost his head all by himself. And I think we can be certain that some of our former comrades will continue to attack and murder without really knowing why, and kill off the Red Brigades' declaration without the need for dirty tricks to push them into crime.'

'The right can't just blame the violence on a bunch of gun-toting individuals as they always do. They're bound to try, I grant you, but it could well be too late. There are good reasons to hurry.'

'What reasons?'

'Two months ago, in January, the ultra-right extremists who planted the bomb in Piazza Fontana were cleared. Seventeen dead. No culprits. Insufficient evidence.'

'I don't see the connection.'

'The Piazza Fontana massacre was the first in a long series, carried out with the backing of the secret service, whose aim was clearly to destabilise the country.'

'I know it, you know it, everyone knows it.'

'That's all very well. But when they start clearing the names of known killers, authors of such a historically significant massacre, twenty years after the event, the right needs to divert attention while it gets its house in order.'

'Operation whitewash has been underway for a while. Nothing new there.'

'Yes, but it's very much in the news because, after the Piazza Fontana killers in January, it'll be the turn of the *Italicus* train killers in September, then those of the Brescia massacre before the year's out. Same protagonists, the Ordine Nuovo fascists, same victims, same aims. And the same outcomes to the trials: they'll all be whitewashed. If the farce is repeated too often, it'll end up by not being funny any more. A distraction has to be found, and immediately. Give the press and public opinion something else to think about.'

Roberto looked out of the window, a big square of blue sky, so blue, so calm. He speaks without turning round.

'I admire you for your ability to think and rationalise. I have to say that I'm not able to. Not yet. Right now I'm too stunned by Carlo's death. I feel as though I'm at the bottom of a hole.'

'Don't you know the Roma saying? When you're at the bottom of a hole and sinking, stop digging.'

10 March

It is dark by the time Lisa arrives home, exhausted after a stressful day at work. She had to make up her four days' absence, four days in mourning. Piles of reports to type, appointments to rearrange, telephone ringing nonstop, no time to think about Carlo, even during the lunch hour. Now, all she wants is a hot shower, a coffee with buttered bread, and bed. She climbs the four flights of stairs puffing, rummages in her bag for her keys, and stumbles over a young man sitting outside her front door, asleep, his head on his arms resting on his knees. Intrigued, she wakes him. He looks up. A shock. In the wan light of the staircase, the photo from the newspaper, the adolescent face of the young hoodlum. She feels her legs buckle. Pushing him aside, she hurriedly puts her key in the lock, opens the door and says to him in Italian: 'Come in, I need to sit down.'

Lisa sinks into a chair leaving him standing there awkwardly, his eyes widening at the sight of so many books. Two walls are lined with bookshelves, and piles of books are scattered everywhere – on the floor, by the bed, on the furniture. Her eyes closed, her hands covering her face, Lisa takes a moment to regain her composure. To his credit, the boy waits, keeping quiet and showing no sign of impatience. When she opens her eyes again, she looks at him. He looks very young, with tattered clothes, a mobile, elusive face, tousled dark hair. She motions to him to sit in the other armchair facing her. When he is settled, his body rigid and his hands crossed, he says to her: 'My name is Filippo Zuliani and I'm a friend of Carlo's.'

'I know who you are. I've read the papers. What are you doing here?' He takes an envelope from a side pocket on his bag and holds it out to her. She reads her own name, Lisa Biaggi, and her address in Rue de Belleville. With a pang, she recognises Carlo's handwriting. She does not touch the envelope.

'So what are you trying to prove to me?'

The kid – because he is a kid – looks disconcerted. He has not anticipated this kind of a reaction. He hesitates and puts the envelope down on the coffee table.

'You'd better begin at the beginning. Your escape. Why did the two of you escape?'

'Why?' His surprise wasn't an act. 'Because in prison you're always trying to escape.'

'Let's keep this simple: how? Give me the details, please.'

Filippo pauses. He has been expecting this moment. Carlo had said, 'Tell Lisa'. Since making the decision to head for Paris, he has replayed the scenes from his story, prepared himself to tell Lisa everything. And now, she is there in front of him. Not the warm, welcoming woman he had imagined. With her fine features, she is beautiful, for sure, but glacial. There is no going back now. He embarks on his story without looking at her, keeping his mind focused on what he is saying.

'I was Carlo's cellmate from the day I arrived in prison, seven months ago. I liked him from the start. I don't know how he felt. Over time, he probably grew to like me. You always end up liking the people who admire you, I think. We used to talk every night, him about Milan, the seventies. I didn't have much to talk about since I hadn't had much of a life before prison. In any case, not a life I'm proud of. But he was proud. He refused to join any of the workshops, and he hardly ever came out of our cell. I told him about my work, the day-to-day life of the prison, all the goings-on – it gave me something to talk about, and it entertained him. I was part of the cleaning team, and one of my jobs was to clean the bin room where a big rubbish chute emptied the waste from the whole wing into two big skips. The full skips were collected at the same time every day by a truck. Half an hour after the truck had come by, it was my job to pick up any rubbish that had fallen on the ground while the skips were being hoisted up, then wash down the area. I would tell Carlo about the filth, the heat, the stench. The bin room was tiny, completely closed in by a metal shutter. When the sun beat down on it the waste fermented, and it really stank. But he didn't give a shit about my working conditions, he was only interested in the width of the rubbish chute. Could a man fit into it? I told him that in my opinion, a man could easily slide down it. From that moment on, the pair of us began to dream. He asked me to find the entrance to the chute, which I located behind the canteen kitchen, on the first floor. Then Carlo signed up for the canteen dishwashing team. I put out feelers to find out what time the trucks came by, but the timing didn't fit. My shift needed to be half an hour later to coincide with when Carlo was on the dishwashing detail and I was in the bin room. But he told me not to worry, that he'd find a solution on the day.

I trusted him, I didn't ask any questions. My job was to find out the procedure for searching the skips leaving the prison, and I got that information easily. The searches were perfunctory to say the least. Two guards lifted the tarpaulin covering the skip and gave it a quick once-over, and that was it. So we decided to go for it. Carlo set the date. That day, when I went into the bin room, I saw the skips were still full and I knew we were really going to do it. My heart was racing until I heard the trucks turning into the yard, half an hour later than usual. I checked that the chute was in the right position, and before the big main gate opened, I gave the signal by banging five times on the side. Carlo was in the canteen on the first floor, he must have been waiting by the mouth of the chute, and at the signal he dived down it. He shot out into the skip like a cannon ball. The main gate opened, the trucks were about to drive in. I grabbed the top of the skip, did an acrobatic flipover and dived in, landing next to him. We swam down to the bottom of the skip through the rubbish bags. Then, we waited, listened, breathing as shallowly as possible so as not to suffocate. For how long, it's impossible to say. But not all that long. Then we were tipped out of the skip on to a rubbish dump. That's it.' He stopped, apparently exhausted, and finally looked at Lisa. Told like that, it sounded incredibly easy. Another pause. 'It's our story, and now I'm telling it for the first time.'

Lisa is moved, exasperated, and suspicious. First of all, she must calm down. She rises, turning her back on Filippo and potters about in the galley kitchen. She never cooks – no room, no time, no desire. But she does have a cupboard with a few emergency supplies. Right now, busying herself affords her a degree of composure and the time to think things through. His story is too polished. Well, he's had the time to replay the film over and over again, it's true. She returns with a dish of tortellini in broth, which she sets down on the coffee table in front of him. He pounces on it. Lisa watches him then, when he has finished eating, she says aggressively:

'Nothing you've told me explains how you ended up on my doorstep.'

'As soon as we were tipped out with all the rubbish, we stood up.'

He pauses for a second, recalling the sudden feeling of panic at finding himself standing on top of that mound of refuse. *What the fuck am I doing here? I should never have jumped into that skip.* He had felt like crying. He clears his throat: 'There was a ladder against the wall. On the other side, a car was waiting for us. We lay down side by side on the floor in the back, and the car drove off at speed, over very bumpy roads. I got banged around, and I'm sure Carlo did too. I think I blacked out at times, it's a bit hazy.'

'Who was driving the car?'

'I'm not sure. No one I knew. A guy at the wheel and a girl next to him, that's all I could see.'

'A girl?'

'Yes, a girl, I'm certain of that.'

'And you weren't able to see the guy or the girl? At any time? Didn't they say anything?'

'No, nothing. They didn't open their mouths while I was there. And I couldn't see anything because the driver had turned up the collar of his coat and was wearing dark glasses. The girl had her collar turned up too, and wore a headscarf. They never turned round to look at me.'

'And then what?'

'The car stopped somewhere in the mountains, by a ruin, a sort of barn. Carlo took me aside. He gave me a bag...' Filippo jerks his thumb at the canvas bag beside him on the chair, '... already packed with two sandwiches, clothes and some money, and he said, "This is where we part company. I have things to do. I'll meet you in Milan in a month's time. Meanwhile, stay out of sight, and if things get too difficult here in Italy, head for Paris. Go to this address, tell the woman I sent you, and tell her our story. She'll help you." Those were his precise words: *"If things get too difficult"*. I only realised later what he meant. And then the three of them got into another car that was hidden in the barn, and they drove off.'

'And you still hadn't caught a glimpse of the other two?'

'Vaguely, from a distance, and only from behind.'

'Did you know who I was? Had Carlo told you about me?'

'No, never.'

In silence, she lets that sink in. *A girl was waiting for him when he broke out, and he never mentioned me to his cellmate, during six months of cohabiting.* Careful. A trap.

'Did he give you any addresses in Milan?'

'No. Just the name of a youth hostel. After a month, I was supposed to go there and wait until he contacted me. Later on I forgot the name.'

'So what did you do next, after Carlo left and you were on your own?'

'I set off on foot over the mountains, heading for Milan. I walked for days, taking care to follow disused footpaths. And then I arrived in Bologna. It was the first city I set foot in after our escape.' Pause, his voice choked. 'I bought the paper, and I found out … It was a shock. There's no other word to describe it, a shock.' He runs his hand over his face. 'Then I felt empty. What was I going to do in Milan? A city I don't know … and then, I suddenly felt frightened, very frightened. We broke out together … I'd vanished for three weeks … and during that time, I'd seen no one and no one had seen me. No possible alibi. My photo was in the papers after the escape: the cops were saying they had a lead, and that could only be me. A bank robbery, and now a *carabiniere* and a security guard dead. Carlo had said, "If things get too difficult, go and see her." Things got too difficult, so here I am.'

Lisa retreats into silence. She is disconcerted by these echoes of Carlo alive arriving out of the blue. She tries to get her bearings, something to hold on to. Is his story credible? Maybe, maybe not. In any case it doesn't contradict her last phone conversation with Carlo. A joint escape in which the kid has a secondary but necessary role. Does he or doesn't he know who the real accomplices are? If he does know them, caution will probably prevent him from saying so. Carlo was able to get rid of him by arranging to meet up in Milan, without implicating anyone else, without revealing any addresses, and with no intention of turning up. "*Don't worry. My cellmate and I have already parted company.*" A month gave him time to go underground if he was worried about the kid informing on him. Not a very honourable thing to do if the kid was clean, but a possible, even likely, course of action. The truly painful thing is the disclosure that during those months of intimacy with Filippo, Carlo never once mentioned her. *He never spoke about me. That girl in the car.* A crazy pang of jealousy. She rises, picks up Filippo's dirty plate and puts it in the sink. *Don't let yourself go. Seven years inside, that changes a man, that's what Roberto was trying to tell me. He spent the last months of his life in close confinement with this kid, but his death is part of our shared history, his and mine. And I won't let go of it.* She brings a plate of biscuits over to the table, sets it down, takes one and eats it to give herself time. Then she says: 'Carlo was set up. He was assassinated by a crack marksman, *Carabiniere* Lucio Renzi, lying in wait for him inside the bank. And you're to blame for that assassination.'

Filippo is taken aback.

'Me?'

'Yes, you.'

'I don't get it.'

She looks at him with barely contained fury.

'You put the idea into his head and gave him the means to escape. If he'd stayed in jail, he'd still be alive. And eventually he'd have been released, sooner or later.'

She slowly regains her self-control. *He's just a kid in rags, unable to get his breath back, disoriented. Not to blame for too much. Calm down. Mustn't get carried away, it's beneath me.* She looks away.

'Sorry. I'm deeply distressed by Carlo's death. I spoke out of turn, so don't take any notice. I'm exhausted and I have to be at work early tomorrow. You can sleep here, and we can talk it all over in the morning. You use the bathroom first, while I make up a bed for you in here.'

11 March

Filippo has an appointment with a woman he doesn't know, in a swanky part of Neuilly. Lisa gave him some money to buy himself some clean clothes and said, 'Here's the address. She's a friend of mine, and she's agreed to rent you her studio apartment. Goodbye and good luck.' Not a word more, no explanation. He walks down a street that stinks of the bourgeoisie, the establishment. He has a strong impulse to run away as fast as he can, as far as possible, but doesn't have the guts. Where would he go? He keeps walking until he reaches number 18. A small, soulless, modern apartment block. Marble and mirrors in the lobby, dark wood and mirrors in the lift. Sixth floor. He rings the bell. The door opens, he is expected. A woman in her forties, magnificent as Italian women of that age are – tall, erect, curvaceous, golden-brown eyes in an open face, a dazzling smile. And a mass of coppery blonde hair like the girl in the mountains who had smiled at Carlo, and whose fleeting image had left an indelible impression on Filippo's imagination. A crazy hope, the warmth of an older sister, lover, mother. Come all the way to Paris to find her and love her. She extends her hand, a rapid, all-purpose handshake, a formality, hopes dashed. Perhaps her smile's a mask. She speaks to him in Italian: 'Filippo? I'm Cristina Pirozzi. I was expecting you, come in.'

She shows him into quite a spacious hall, furnished with an elaborately carved Italian wardrobe, a huge, antique mirror, a magnificent grandfather clock and a Persian rug on the floor. Two doors facing each other. Cristina opens one of them.

'This is the studio flat I mentioned to Lisa.'

A large, well-lit room, French window opening on to a balcony, glass-and-steel guardrail, good-quality, simple furniture, a big bookcase full of books, a bathroom and a tiny galley kitchen. And four big clothes cupboards, for him, whose only luggage is his canvas bag.

'It was my son's place, but he lives in New York now. Ever since Giorgio, my partner, left, I've lived alone in this huge apartment.' A pause. 'Does it suit you?' He stammers. 'Here are the keys. I arranged everything with Lisa. In theory the rent is 400 francs a month, all-in and cash, but of course you can pay me when you've got a job. My phone number's on the kitchen table in case you have any problems.'

And she leaves.

Filippo finds himself alone, broken, drained. *What the hell was I expecting, for God's sake?* He sits down on the bed, which is covered with a brightly coloured patchwork counterpane, his shoulders hunched, his arms dangling. He casts his eye over the bookshelves where there is a mix of French and Italian books. Yet another library, like at Lisa's. All these books he hasn't read. He walks over to the shelves and touches the spines. If he wants to read, which book should he start with? A name comes back to him: Victor Hugo, Carlo used to say. 'A Victor Hugo to tell our epic tale.' How is he to find that name among all these books? He scans the spines – names, titles that mean nothing to him, seemingly arranged at random. Crestfallen. *They're all telling me: you don't fit in here, we're prepared to help you, then bye-bye. Cristina made that perfectly clear. She called me Filippo, my first name, no surname, she stood in the hall to talk to me, as if I was some kind of a servant. Put the money for the rent in the hall cupboard – avoid contact at all costs. Then, all condescending, 'I arranged everything with Lisa.' She didn't look at me once, I was invisible, non-existent.* A memory surfaces: *I was invisible for Carlo, too. He said, 'my escape', a memory immediately blocked out, buried again. Don't think about it any more, too painful, forget. Lisa, Cristina, all their books that I'll never read. I'm a pawn and these two women are just playing with me.* Resentment. He feels the urge to run away again. And to take the rug and the mirror with him. Not the clock, too cumbersome. He will have no trouble selling them at a flea market on the outskirts, they must have them here, and then he can do a runner and find his friends in Rome, with enough money to swagger about, at least for a few days. And treat himself to two or three girls – he can show these women he is not intimidated by them. *In my dreams. I'm forgetting that I'm wanted by the cops for two murders. But I'm also forgetting I can no longer stand the life of a squatter in Rome. Be honest just for once. My arrest was actually a relief – I wasn't able to cut loose, didn't have the balls, no future. The cops did me a favour. Those days are over. End of. Grit your teeth and get used to being alone.* He removes his shoes, lies down on the bed and falls asleep.

12 March

Every Sunday there is a weekly meeting of the Italian refugees in France. It's a sort of rallying point, an informal gathering, people come when they can, to breathe the air of home and indulge in a little nostalgia. The discussions are sometimes highly political, all the major decisions affecting the refugees are thrashed out here with the lawyers who attend regularly to maintain close contact with the little community. The gathering also acts as a mutual support group – people pass on tips for finding a job, a place to stay in another city, and help each other out. And they drink Italian wine. They also tear one another apart; the divisions between the various exiled ultra-leftist groups are as acrimonious today as they had been in Italy, and heated arguments often break out, with people dispersing into small groups. It is more like gossiping than a political debate, but no one questions the vital importance of this fixed point to help them cope with life in exile. And the same applies to Lisa, too. She has always known that one day she will have to go back there and talk about Carlo's death. Today, she feels strong enough to do that. She even needs to – it is a way of making his death official, the first step in coming to terms with it.

Roberto picks her up from her place and takes her for lunch at Le Pacific, a big Chinese restaurant close by, on the corner of Rue de Belleville – a light, quick meal. He senses that she is at breaking point and is worried, watching her every movement. He orders dumplings and iced tea; he knows what she likes. Attentive as the lover he might have been, years ago, had it not been for the handsome Carlo, who had the kudos of being a factory-worker – back when that counted. Roberto, though, had always looked like a white-collar worker, and was beginning to go bald – he had stood no chance. Now the field is clear, but it is way too late. All that remains between them is affection.

The Sunday afternoon meetings are held in a big room lent by a French association. A stark, shabby decor, grey-tiled floor, bare walls painted a grubby yellow, harsh light, and stacking chairs. But on a table in a corner is a buffet, with cold drinks, wine, cakes and two thermos flasks of coffee, all on a fine red tablecloth with a bunch of pink flowers. They have been told that Lisa is coming. Someone has brought two bottles of Spumante. A party wine. To console themselves for Carlo's death, or to celebrate it? Who knows? Thirty or so people are waiting for her to arrive, chatting noisily in small groups that form and break up according to personal and political affinities. The same question is on everyone's lips: what tone will Lisa set for the meeting? *Mater dolorosa*, or robust defence of the hero? Some are placing bets.

Lisa enters the room and a hush falls. Everyone remains still, waiting for her first move, her first words. She appears to falter, then makes up her mind, smiles, greets everyone, handshakes, embraces. The noise swells again, people come over to express their condolences, looking grief-stricken, some more genuinely so than others. Roberto leaves her and goes over to one of the lawyers, sitting slightly aloof, near the buffet.

Lisa quickly cuts short the expressions of sympathy, holds on to the back of a chair for support with both hands, and begins to speak in a clear, composed voice.

'After his escape, I spoke to Carlo on the telephone.' Surprised, the audience waits in silence for more detail, but she gives none. 'He told me that he endorsed the declaration by the former leaders of the Red Brigades, and now felt freed from any obligation to continue the struggle in prison. He was planning to get hold of some money and fake ID – without taking any risks, he was insistent on that point – so he could go abroad and start a new life. He didn't say any more.' She pauses, the audience is still rapt. 'I'm convinced he was the victim of a sting set up to discredit the entire far left and make us look like a bunch of dangerous common criminals. He was assassinated by Brigadier Lucio Renzi who hid inside the bank and then shot him. I consider it my duty to fight to the bitter end and find out what really happened that day, and make sure that Carlo doesn't go down in history as the leader of a useless gang and a failed bank robber.'

Lisa stops, choked with emotion. The silence is broken by an anonymous female voice: 'You seem very certain that this battle is worth fighting. I'm not. Carlo isn't the only Red Brigades survivor who's carried on shooting anyone and anything, tarring us all with the same brush, including those of us who were against your reckless choice to take up arms.'

Lisa wavers briefly. *Whatever you do, don't argue, not now, keep calm.* She goes on, in a measured tone:

'Yes, I'm fighting to protect Carlo's memory because he was my man, and because I'm devastated by his death. But that's not the only reason. I want to convince you that he wasn't the only one to be set up, that the sting is part of a wider strategy to discredit our struggle, the entire non-parliamentary far left, whether we are pro armed struggle or not. Let's make no mistake, our destinies are now bound together. If we don't stand side by side and fight to preserve our past, we'll lose the battle all over again, and we'll be erased from the history of the struggle in Italy. And that's why I am counting on the help – on the collaboration – of all of you to shine a light on what really happened outside the Piemonte-Sardegna bank.'

A murmur ripples through the gathering. Clearly opinion is extremely divided. Lisa continues in the same vein: 'I'm looking for all the information we can find on this Lucio Renzi, Carlo's killer. Ask around, ask any journalists you know, any contacts you still have in Italy. Who is he, where does he come from? I'm sure we'll find something. Thank you, all of you, for your help.'

Lisa pauses for a moment, people are growing restless, some go over and pour themselves a drink or start chatting to their neighbours. When the hubbub dies down, Lisa takes the floor again: 'There's something I must tell you. A week after Carlo was killed, his cellmate, the criminal who escaped with him, turned up at my place.' She has the audience's attention again. 'Apparently Carlo gave him my address. I say "apparently", because, instinctively, I distrust him, but I have no concrete reason to. Everything he's told me so far fits with what I know from other sources. I've put his case in the hands of our lawyers.' The audience turns to the lawyer, who nods. 'I've found him a job as a night watchman and a studio flat that he's subletting from a work colleague of mine. I owe it to Carlo's memory to help him, and I feel I've done all I can. I'm quits. Let me know if you'd like him to come to our Sunday meetings, and I'll give you his contact details. I repeat, I'm not keen, I don't trust this guy, but it's up to you. That's all from me, thank you for being here, and for your support and help.'

Lisa sits down, suddenly exhausted, her gaze vacant. People avoid her, forming little knots again by the buffet. There are heated arguments in hushed voices. The lawyer pours himself a glass of fruit juice and leans over to Roberto: 'Do you believe this business about Carlo being set up?'

'No, but I believe that Lisa needs to believe in it to cope with Carlo's death. She's never stopped waiting for him.'

A woman called Chiara sidles up to Roberto, leans close to him and murmurs with pinched lips: 'Lisa's the only person here who believes her story. That arsehole was capable of wrecking our lives singlehandedly. He didn't need anyone's help. And you know it as well as I do.'

Roberto turns his back on her, without replying.

Further away Giovanni, a stocky man in his fifties, is holding forth, surrounded by three women who are lapping up his words, spoken in a half-tone: 'I've had enough of her noble widow act, her scout-leader airs, the way she flaunts her generosity, her posturing, as if she were the custodian of the memory of all the radical struggles in Italy. We know as much as she does about all that, if not more. And her ridiculous stories. She's been in France for too long. Exile creates fantasists and paranoia.'

CHAPTER THREE

MARCH 1987–FEBRUARY 1988, LA DÉFENSE, PARIS

Night watchman at the Tour Albassur, at La Défense. The walk from the Métro exit to the staff entrance is an ordeal repeated nightly. Filippo strides across the deserted concourse, his head down. Aim: to avoid being crushed by the office blocks lined up like soldiers, dizzyingly high, threatening, blocking out the sky. Blasts of freezing or scorching-hot air. The few grey shapes scuttling soundlessly in various directions no longer seem human.

Ten p.m. Filippo begins his shift. He checks in at the security guards' office, a long, narrow, windowless room on the ground floor, crammed with machines and CCTV screens, just behind the magnificent reception desks in the foyer. He picks up his badge and greets his colleague, his sole companion for the entire night, an elderly man who's been given this job by Albassur so they won't have to fire him three years before he is due to retire. He's a sociable type and seems genuinely sorry not to be able to communicate with Filippo, who doesn't yet speak a word of French.

Then Filippo sets off on his evening tour to inspect all the floors. The same ritual every night. Lift. Stop at the first floor. The light timer switches on, Filippo exits the lift and scans his fob into a little device on the wall. Three sets of double doors, one to his left, one to his right and one straight ahead of him. Start with the doors on the right, according to his instructions. He pushes them open. A long corridor, wanly lit by the glow from the luminous emergency exit signs. He advances slowly along the corridor, on thick carpet, not a sound, not a living soul, the sensation of walking on cotton wool. Office doors to his left, office doors to his right, all identical. He opens them, closes them, repetitive actions. A lounge area with vending machines, a coffee machine, and two imitation-leather armchairs. Deserted, sinister. At the far end of the corridor, a large boardroom, and the scanner. He swipes his fob. Return to the lifts. Swing doors, left-hand corridor, scanner, return, central corridor, scanner, back again. Lift, second floor. Each floor, one after another. There are thirty-two floors in this block. Sometimes a floor of offices with a view, less claustrophobic perhaps than the long corridors, but the loneliness there is overwhelming, chilling.

Thirty-second floor, the last. The space is designed in a much less regular fashion, the offices are much bigger, but there is still a scanner, and the loneliness. Filippo goes into the boardroom. A dim light, like everywhere else. He skirts the oval table in the centre of the room, hemmed with wood-and-leather chairs, and stops in front of the vast bay window that runs the entire length of the room. He stands stock still, digesting the shock he feels every night. He is mesmerised, overcome by the view, as he had been by the white rocky ridge, the blue lake and the immense sky in the mountains when he was on the run. On either side, within touching distance, at the same height as him, loom the dark shapes of the neighbouring towers, punctuated by a few lines and pinpoints of light, and just opposite him, a large gap affording a view of Paris. The lines and shapes are clear and sharp – the deep, dark course of the Seine, the lighter black mass of the Bois de Boulogne, the Eiffel Tower with its coppery outline, the epitome of elegance, standing out against the sovereign midnight-blue sky, and the light at the top, its powerful revolving beam mechanically sweeping space. Seen from here, the hasty, oppressive walk across the concourse each night feels like an initiation test before entering dreamland. And each night, confronted with this magnificent landscape built by men but devoid of any trace of life, in solitude and silence, he listens to the words going round and round in his head, the sentences that form all by themselves. He waits patiently for the memory of Guidoriccio to return and haunt him, and each night the warlord turns up. This landscape suits him. He would gladly make it his. Who is Guidoriccio? wonders Filippo. The triumphant warrior in flesh and blood, astride his horse, challenging stone-built cities and deserted fortifications in glorious defiance of all the gods and all men, of whom he dreamed in his childhood. Or the lone horseman, playing at war, without enemies, and therefore without pleasure and without any possibility of victory, whom he had met during his long trek over the Italian mountains? Or is he a lifeless equestrian statue on a stage set? What is this knight's message? Is it that the tempting but fatal combination of solitude and dreams are both his destiny and mine? The presence of this enigmatic character at his side stops Filippo from becoming lost.

The walkie-talkie on his belt crackles. 'Everything OK?' asks a tinny voice. His round is finished, the moment of reverie too; it's time to go back down to the ground floor, to the duty office of the Tour Albassur security team, where the longest part of the night is about to commence.

Night after night, between the evening round after the departure of the last employees and the morning round before the arrival of the 'office cleaning operatives', Filippo finds himself shut up with his colleague in the security guards' office. They sit back-to-back in comfortable swivel armchairs, and they each keep an eye on thirty or so monitors on the opposite wall that relay footage from the CCTV cameras in the offices, the control panels of the alarm systems of the high-security offices, while still others ensure that all the utilities and technical systems are functioning correctly – heating, water pressure, power circuits, along with a dozen telephones. Each guard has a logbook on his desk to report any incidents. Which never occur. Stuck in front of the still, flat, ugly images of the screens blinking and flickering in the emptiness, Filippo feels giddy. Like many night watchmen probably, he fantasises about a disaster that would blur all the screens, set off all the alarms and create a reassuring chaos justifying, for a few minutes, the existence of his job. The temptation to provoke such an incident preys on him briefly before evaporating. His colleague Antoine, on the other hand, keeps himself busy. Unable to converse with Filippo, he flicks through old magazines, does crosswords, eats cake and snoozes.

Filippo soon realises that he needs to find a way of filling his time, otherwise he'll get depressed. Learn French? He tries for a while with an old Assimil method. And discovers that he has no incentive. Who does he want to speak French with? And what for? *Because my future is in France? What future? Before thinking about my future, I'd do better to try and get a grip on my present. The burning question: what am I doing here, far away from everything I know? I'm here because I jumped into that skip. I escaped, without planning to. Why did I jump? What made me do such a senseless thing?*

While his thoughts wander, he has got into the habit of doodling the leaves and scrolls of the acanthus fern – in black pencil, on white sheets of paper. In the near-contemplative silence, his hand is as free as his mind, and his doodles mingle with the rhythm of words. He'd jumped because he'd followed Carlo, like iron filings to a magnet. His thoughts always returned to Carlo. His form, so clear, so close, within reach, a warm glow – Filippo closes his eyes and holds out his hand, as he used to do in their cell, but only encounters emptiness. He hunches over his sheet of paper; his drawings overlap. Above all, Carlo is a voice, a language, and stories. The memories of never-ending nights spent listening to him flood back powerfully, overwhelming him, those memories that he'd tried to bury, to destroy because he felt abandoned, betrayed. Carlo had the words to talk about the struggle of those heady years, the passion, the battle against slave labour, the thrill of the fight, the euphoria of victory, the agony of defeat and the joy of freedom, jubilant violence. Being prepared to put your life at risk, every day. *For a while I wanted to forget everything about him. Betrayal. Impossible.* Filippo is suffocating. The sheet of paper is now covered in black. He screws it into a ball, throws it into the waste-paper bin and picks up another.

Gradually, the words in his head become sentences that fit together. On the page, a series of almost perfect circles overlap, intersect and reinforce one another. *I was blown away by everything Carlo told me; his passion, his hunger for freedom and his violence were the very stuff of my life in Rome, before jail. My horror of my mother's exhausting, humdrum existence, my hatred of my father's submissive, mediocre life, which he blotted out with alcohol to the point where he despised himself, my rebellion against the cops and my teachers, the crushing boredom of village life, and the feeling of not having a grip on anything, not counting for anything or for anyone, drove me to look for adventure among Rome's squats. I wanted to live, but I didn't know it, I'd never had the words to express all that. Never even the desire to express it. Carlo taught me that if I couldn't find the right words to say who I am, I wouldn't exist, not even in my own eyes. With his words, he justified my rebellion and salvaged my Rome years from being no more than a defeat. So naturally I followed him, I jumped into the skip. It was a free and necessary act.*

Filippo stops scribbling, sits up, relaxes, breathes and drinks a glass of water. He has just struck a blow against despair. The overlapping circles covering the entire surface of the page in front of him take on the shape of a crowd of faceless heads. A crowd with no voice. He doesn't throw this sheet away, but puts it carefully to one side for the time being.

After his leap into the skip came separation. At this point, his voice becomes husky, the words stop flowing. A complex tangle of confused feelings. No desire to try and unravel them. Filippo puts it all to the back of his mind. *I'll think about it later.* Then Carlo's death, his own escape, Paris. He recalls his meeting with Lisa, then Cristina. Looking for a shoulder to cry on. A little love. Didn't find it. Lisa's fury. Hatred, the word forms, imposes itself. *She hates me. Why? She told me. Because I'm to blame for Carlo's death, I put the idea into his head and gave him the means to escape. Harsh words. But now, I understand them, I accept them. To blame for his death, OK. What about Cristina? She doesn't hate me, she doesn't even know I exist. For those two women, Carlo's a prince and I'm a piece of shit. They helped me because Carlo asked them to. Fair enough. But Carlo doesn't belong to them. They don't know him. The closeness of being in jail, the breakout, the dangers, the ordeal we went through together, that's our story, Carlo's and mine, not theirs.*

He picks up the sheet of paper with the anonymous crowd on it. With a few pencil strokes he adds Lisa's dark hair, Cristina's chignon, here a look, there a mouth, and their faces emerge and replicate. *Before Carlo died, as he set off for his final battle, he said to me, 'Tell Lisa.' I've got to tell it. How? Put my trust in Carlo, listen to my memories, let his words come out. And when I have my whole story nice and tight ...* he hunches over the sheet of paper and contemplates the faces. *Those two will come to understand that Carlo is mine, not theirs, and that he never did belong to them. A story of men.*

The time for tears is over. He dreams of conquering the two women, the way you conquer a land, for the pleasure of conquering, and then leaving for pastures new.

That day, I went into the bin room to clean it, as I did every day. And I knew that today was the day. The screw who opened the door for me didn't notice that the skip was full, whereas usually it was empty, and he locked the door behind me, as he did every day. I was breathing fast and my hands were clammy. I waited, straining my ears, counting the seconds by my heartbeat. According to our calculations, we had thirty minutes before the alarm would be raised.

After one minute, or a bit more – the minute went on so long – I heard the sound of an engine in the yard. It was the truck come to pick up the skip and take it to the dump. I gave five sharp knocks on the rubbish chute. Carlo was on dishwashing detail in the canteen, on the floor above. He heard the signal that we'd rehearsed over the last few days. He sneaked over to the mouth of the rubbish chute and jumped in. He shot out into the skip like a cannon ball and plunged down, swimming his way to the bottom. Then I jumped too. I grabbed the top of the skip wall, steadied myself and dived in after him. As I jumped, the metal shutter that closed off the bin room from the yard began to open. The guards checked that the room was empty, the truck was about to load the skip. I slid down among the plastic bags, the pressure was crushing, I couldn't tell which way was up or down, and some of the bags had split. I felt something slimy and rough against my face, I wanted to throw up, I could hardly breathe, and I began to panic and choke. Drowning in a sea of rubbish. Carlo's hand grabbed my arm, he brought his face very close to mine, pushed a bag out of the way to give me some air, and whispered, 'Protect your face with your T-shirt, everything's fine.' Then a crash to make us shudder: the skip had been loaded on to the truck. 'Good news,' murmured Carlo, 'we're going to make it.' I got my breath back. We began to manoeuvre ourselves very slowly into an upright position, trying to clear an air pocket around our heads. Carlo guided me.

We had to control our breathing, we knew it was vital otherwise we'd suffocate to death amid the rubbish. The truck started up. Our hands fumbled and found each other, locked. A stop: exit checks, signature of the paperwork, and inspection of the skip by the screws. We knew that it would be cursory, but what if, that day... Hearts thumping. The truck was on its way, we squeezed hands. We waited a few minutes, counting slowly, then bit by bit we fought our way to the surface. When we were able to come up for air, I took a deep breath, despite the smell, then threw up. Carlo was kneeling, he held on to the wall of the skip with one hand, very much in control. I thought how he'd saved my life, in those first few minutes after I'd jumped in. I didn't say anything because Carlo didn't like shows of emotion. But he knew.

The truck slowed down. The driver was Marco, the leader of my gang when I was a thief in Rome, before my arrest. Using a false name, he'd got himself a job as a driver for the subcontractor who handled the prison's rubbish, and the whole operation had been coordinated by his sister Luciana, who often used to come and visit me in jail. We'd been in love, before I got banged up. Or rather, we thought we were. But we were very young. In other words, we used to fuck each other. And she was a great help in planning our escape. It was agreed that we'd jump out when Marco braked three times in quick succession. He couldn't stop because he wasn't alone in the cab. We felt him brake three times, we shot up together, grabbed the side of the skip, heaved ourselves over the edge, hung there for a second, then we let go, throwing ourselves out as far as possible, clear of the truck. We hit the ground hard, but we were ready for it. We both tucked ourselves up into a ball and rolled on to the asphalt. We watched the truck drive off, then we stood up. The place was empty. Good choice. About five hundred metres away were some apartment blocks, one of those suburban housing estates plonked down in the middle of the countryside. We had to hope that no one had seen us jump off the truck, and we still needed a bit of luck. Carlo said to me, 'By my reckoning, we've got ten minutes left before the alarm's raised in the prison.' We had to get away from the route taken by the refuse truck as fast as possible. Ten minutes just might be enough. We crossed the fields very quickly, heading for the apartment block. We kept calm, didn't run, brushing ourselves down to get rid of the rubbish clinging to our hair and our clothes as we went. We walked round the first building and found ourselves in a huge car park between two apartment blocks. It was two o'clock in the afternoon, there weren't many people about. A few days earlier

I'd hidden a piece of wire in my pocket, which I unrolled. I chose a Fiat model that I knew well. Within twenty seconds, I'd opened the door, and thirty seconds later I had the steering lock deactivated and the engine running, and we drove out of the car park. Carlo looked at his watch. 'The alarm's been raised,' he said. We drove away from Rome. We left the stolen car in a supermarket car park around twenty kilometres away, where we waited for Luciana, Marco's sister. She was standing next to her car, against the sunlight, her mass of copper-blond hair glinting in the sun. I found her stunning, but she had eyes only for Carlo. I'd already lost that game.

The three of us embraced and thumped the roof of her car – we'd pulled off our escape. Then we got into the car, I took the wheel, she sat next to me, half-turned towards Carlo sitting like a king on the back seat, and we headed off in the direction of the mountains.

Filippo is absorbed in his work. He is laboriously copying out on to a pad of lined paper, in a careful, legible hand, a text extracted from twenty or so sheets of rough paper covered in crossings-out and corrections, without stopping to glance at the bank of CCTV monitors in front of him. His old colleague is so intrigued that he forgets to watch his television, craning his neck to try and see what Filippo is up to that is so engrossing. When Filippo finally sits up and carefully slips the sheets of paper inside an orange binder, he can no longer contain himself and asks, jerking his thumb in the direction of the binder:

'What are you doing? What's that thing?'

The very question that Filippo has been asking himself since he starting copying out his notes. 'I'm writing.'

'So I can see, but what are you writing?'

Filippo pauses, searches for the words in French, and blurts out an answer that he has clearly been rehearsing: 'I'm writing my story.'

'So you're a writer?'

The bank raid was planned for 3 p.m. on the 3rd of March. On the first of March, Carlo, Pepe and I held a vigil back at camp. Luciana had departed early in the morning, leaving us her car. She had to walk alone for a good three hours over the mountains before finding a car to take her back to Rome, but we men wanted to be on our own. I caressed her mass of copper hair one last time, feeling very emotional, then I went into the barn with Pepe, to allow Carlo to say goodbye to her in private, surrounded by nature.

When he came back, we got out the guns, three Walther P38 pistols. Our final shooting practice, four cartridges each, we didn't have enough ammunition for more. I'd never used firearms in my Rome days, I was wary of them, I didn't like the alternately icy or burning feel of them, they scared me. They were like wild animals that I couldn't tame, but I kept quiet and joined in the shooting, same as the other two. I was no worse, either, once I was over the initial shock. Then we cleaned and greased our weapons, lying disassembled on a table in front of us. Carlo lingered, with a faraway look in his eyes. It was plain that he derived a physical thrill from touching the metal, greasing it, breathing in the special smell of mingled grease and powder. We put the guns away. Then, on the same table we spread out a map of Milan and the surrounding area, a map of the neighbourhood and a sketch showing the bank entrance and the interior.

We didn't plan to go further inside the building. The three of us stood poring over the maps, our shoulders and heads brushing, and sometimes our hands touched. Pepe and I listened while Carlo explained to us in detail, a pencil in his hand, who would do what, and the precise timing of the operation. 'Precision is crucial,' Carlo said. 'Our organisation must be flawless.' We were attentive, very solemn. We exchanged a word, a look, our movements were coordinated, we were experiencing an intense moment of comradeship. Then, when the maps were put away, we decided that the fine-tuning was done, and we broke bread. 'Last meal before the battle,' Carlo said, and we shivered with anticipation, fear and pleasure. Afterwards, we found it difficult to chat idly so we sat in silence, and the time dragged. We went to bed early, and took sleeping pills.

Next day, on the second of March, the three of us drove up to Milan in the car that Luciana had left us, the guns hidden under the seats. When we got there, we staked out the area around the bank, to get a clear picture in our minds, then Carlo took the bag with the guns. We dumped the car in a car park, as planned, so that Luciana could pick it up that evening, and we hid in an empty apartment that belonged to friends of Carlo's. For the sake of having something to do, something to say, we went over the next day's schedule twice. Carlo emphasised that as long as we followed the plan to the letter, as long as there were no cock-ups, everything would be fine, they'd be waiting for us – those were his words. And he didn't elaborate any further. The day dragged by very slowly.

The third of March. At last. The day that was to decide our fates. Things started speeding up. We split up. Pepe went to hire two vans and parked them near the bank. My job was to check the condition of the two motorbikes in the garage. I lavished attention on them and drove them to the two positions identified the previous day, so that we could make our getaway in two different directions after the robbery. And then there was more hanging around. I wasn't able to eat the sandwich I'd bought.

We met up in a café a few hundred metres from the bank. Carlo had brought the guns in a sports holdall, we took one each. At 14.30, we got into our vans, Carlo alone in one, Pepe and me in the other. At 14.50, Pepe started up the van and parked it over a driveway to the left of the bank, obstructing the entire pavement. The bike was there, shielded by the van, and I was relieved to see it. At 14.57, the security van drew up in front of the bank and two guards got out, one of them was carrying two bags, the other kept his hand on his hip, on his open holster, and they went into the bank. Just then, Carlo's van pulled up on the driveway to the right of the bank, facing ours. I was very focused, but not frantic, not even anxious; we simply needed to stick to the plan. Carlo opened his door, I opened mine. I didn't take my eyes off him, he was our chief, we took our cue from him. He had his gun in his hand, I picked up mine, but then everything went wrong, and I don't understand how or why. I saw Carlo collapse in slow motion, like in a film. It was impossible, unthinkable, and I lost all sense of reality. I was in another dimension. I'd gone deaf, I couldn't hear a sound, I didn't hear the shots. I turned towards the entrance to the bank, still in slow motion, and I saw a *carabiniere* aiming his gun at me, and one of the security guards taking his gun out extremely slowly. I didn't have the sense that I was in danger, I shot without making the decision to do so, without grasping what was happening. I saw two cops stagger and fall in a muffled silence. I existed only through the gun I was holding with both hands, through my fingers squeezing the trigger. Pepe grabbed me by the arm, brutally, and dragged me from the scene. He shoved me behind the van and started up the bike. I clambered on behind him, clung on to his shoulders, and within a few seconds we were out of sight. I could feel the bike throbbing, I could hear the sound of the engine, I put my gun in my pocket and I could feel the barrel burning my thigh. Gradually I came back down to earth. I replayed the whole scene in my mind, much more clearly than I had experienced it. Three things were certain: Carlo was dead. Dead. I would never hear him talking about his former battles again, inventing his future and mine. Dead without a goodbye, a last outburst, a last caress. Another certainty: I had killed, I'd become a killer, without yet comprehending the full import of those words, the consequences of those actions. And finally: yes, Carlo was right, they'd been waiting for us.

Filippo adds these sheets to those in the orange binder sitting on the desk in front of him. He is concentrating, his elbows on the desk, his face cupped in his hands. The two key sections of his story, the opening and the closing scenes, are written, they exist. His task now is to fill in the bits in between, bring alive the entire story by fleshing it out. How to go about it?

He draws a box in the top left-hand corner of a blank sheet of paper, and writes 'Escape' in it. In the bottom right-hand corner, a box with 'Bank raid'. Three weeks to get from one to the other. Three characters, Carlo, Marco, Luciana, and a fourth, Filippo, the chronicler, slightly in the background, an observer until the final shootout. He scribbles and he thinks. When he feels that he has a scene where something is really happening between the four of them, he gives it a name, a number, and hangs it on the line between the breakout and the bank robbery. Sometimes, he moves a box up or down the line, inserts another. At first, the game amuses him, but soon he is hooked. It is not long before he has the bare bones of his entire story:

After the breakout, the two fugitives and Luciana made it to a ruined farmhouse in the mountains. Marco, the small-time boss from Rome, was waiting for them there. He'd thought of everything, organised everything to enable them to hide out and survive – clothes, food and a few books for Carlo, who appreciated his thoughtfulness. But Marco never did anything for free. He immediately informed them that he had big plans. He wanted to expand his gang and consolidate his territory in Rome. To do that, he'd already done a deal with the local mafia bosses. He needed competent, reliable men, men he could count on, like Carlo and Filippo. Carlo was hesitant and asked for some time to think about it before making a decision. Marco reluctantly agreed, gave Carlo a week and went back to Rome. Luciana stayed at the barn and became Carlo's mistress. Filippo accepted this situation, which he'd known was inevitable ever since they'd first met in the car park. If he was annoyed with Luciana, it was for depriving him of precious moments of intimacy with Carlo rather than for being unfaithful to him. Carlo got back in contact with his Milan friends, those who weren't dead or in jail. To survive, they formed a little band of thieves and lived off run-of-the-mill burglaries, while cultivating the memory of 'the years of fire'.

Carlo trusted former comrades rather than anyone else. He was keen to hold on to his independence, and was instinctively wary of Marco. He suggested that the Milanese should build a solid team, that they should stop being amateurs and move up a gear – first of all, do a bank robbery, in the style of the best of them in the old days. Then, they'd see, they'd have money, the means to plan for the future. The idea soon took shape. The bank was selected, the plans for the raid drawn up. All the logistics were entrusted to the Milan crew. Carlo would head the action group. He came back to the farmhouse with Pepe, one of the Milanese. Filippo, who'd been a pickpocket and bag-snatcher, let himself be sucked in, fascinated by Carlo's eloquent tales of past exploits and his future plans. He would be the third man. Preparations for the robbery were steaming ahead. Marco felt he was losing control of the group and his grand plans were compromised. However, he did seem willing to make a deal: in exchange for his past help, he insisted that the first bank raid take place in Rome, on his turf, so that he could control the share-out. Carlo refused; he insisted on Milan, his home town, on his turf. Neither trusted the other. Besides, claimed Carlo, plans were too far advanced in the north now to change targets. Conflict.

Filippo delights in imagining the clash between the two men, he knows he'll enjoy writing it even more. Carlo, tall, slim, elegant, classy, icily polite, with perfect self-control. Then Marco, squat, burly, a square mug, deep-set eyes and very black, bushy eyebrows in a slash across his forehead, a scar down his left cheek that disfigures his face slightly – a souvenir of knife fights in the turf wars around Termini station – his thuggish manner and brutal gestures. A persistent memory – the mug of the getaway car driver. Filippo counts on writing to help him purge the fear he felt on meeting his gaze, back in the mountains.

Class won out over violence. At least for the time being. Marco seemed to give in. Bank robbery, fiasco. Certainty: Marco grassed on Carlo. Who informed him, day by day, of Carlo's plans, who gave him the means to betray him? Luciana, of course.

The friend more faithful than the woman. Posthumous revenge. Can't let that betrayal go unpunished. Filippo adds another box after the bank robbery, by way of an epilogue.

Filippo, aided by Pepe, kills Marco. The end.

It feels as if his story will hold up and, as to the question 'why has he ended up as night watchman in a tower at La Défense?' he also has an answer that will hold water. Assuming he manages to unravel the yarn right to the end, that is. All he has to do is to write.

As of now, Filippo's days, asleep and awake, are peopled with intrusive characters and snatches of dialogue, all of which never leave him alone for a moment. And his nights, between security rounds, are entirely devoted to writing. He works relentlessly, revises, edits and deletes until he is satisfied he has found the right word, the one that pins down a fleeting thought. Right now, he feels something akin to happiness.

January
Marco has just died, during a fairly confusing turf war between Milanese and Romans, shot perhaps by Pepe. Or Filippo. The story ends there. For the author, it is a visceral certainty – it's over. Full stop, no prisoners. He doesn't want to know why, and he puts down his pen. So, he has come to the end of his endeavour. It isn't going to be easy. He thought he would jump for joy, or do a dance – it's done, it's finished, I've got to the end, success. But not at all. After ten months of a lone undertaking verging on madness, ten months of it consuming all of his energy and of living intensely day and night through Carlo and Filippo, who are him and not him, the last line written, his characters abandon him, disintegrate, and he crumbles, the lifeblood sucked out of him. His brain is exhausted and empty, his body gives way like elastic slackening. For a few days he relishes this state of emptiness, and replenishes his energy.

And then, inevitably, the machine for churning out ideas and emotions starts up again, softly at first. The satisfaction of having managed to explain why and how he's ended up in this windowless room in the Tour Albassur. Nothing either mediocre or risky, but a path of flesh and blood, of violence and freedom which fulfils him. But very soon, the sense of frustration inevitably returns with a vengeance.

I know very well why I'm here. But if I stay stuck in this windowless office in the bowels of a tower in La Défense as a night watchman, I'll be giving Filippo a pathetic end. Who's going to read my amazing tale? No one, not even Antoine, who doesn't understand Italian. So what's the point of all this effort? I didn't just write it for myself, did I? I wrote it so that Lisa could read it, and be hurt by it. To make her understand that I exist, as much as Carlo, and alongside him. Will I have the guts to take my pile of paper to her and put the pages in her hands? I haven't seen that woman in the ten months I've been living in France, but I've felt her burning hatred, like an animal lurking between the two of us. Of course not. And if I did, since she's clever enough to realise that I'm stealing Carlo from her, she's strong and determined enough to burn the manuscript. If I want her to read it, to be forced to read it, there's only one way, and that is to publish it as a book. An object, that will live through its readers and so become indestructible. Like those piles of books at Lisa's place, at Cristina's, in the studio apartment that's my home, all around me. A book, written by me, who's hardly ever read anything. One hell of a revenge. Becoming a writer. 'You are a writer,' Antoine said, seeing me scribbling. Since then, I haven't been able to stop thinking about it. A way of giving my Filippo a life worthy of him, in the world of cultured people, not hoodlums? And in the world of women like Lisa and Cristina, beautiful, desirable, unattainable. It was seeing their faces emerge from my doodling that made me decide to write, wasn't it? See it through to the end. Now that the story is written, I've got to publish it. But how the hell do I go about that?

The question goes round and round in his head for a few days, a few nights. One thing is clear – he won't be able to manage it on his own. He needs a friend in the book world, the world of other people, to act as go-between and introduce him. Who could do that? In Paris, the choice is limited, and it doesn't take long to run through the list of people he knows who may be able to help. Go through Lisa? Don't even think about it. The Italian refugees' lawyers? Only met them once. The memory still smarts – they were so stuck-up and condescending. '*Let us know if you have any problems. We act on behalf of political refugees, not criminals like you, but since Lisa sent you, we'll see what we can do.*' No point. Cristina? He recalls how she'd dazzled him on their first meeting, her beauty, her elegance, her smile. And then his hopes shattered. The impersonal handshake, '*I arranged everything with Lisa,*' and Filippo, anonymous, no surname, just a first name, who had no say in the matter, the rent in cash in an envelope left on a shelf in the hall wardrobe, a few rare, fleeting encounters on the landing. '*Hello*', '*Good evening*', and then nothing. He had always put her in the same camp as Lisa. But he recalls her mass of copper hair and her smile, the same as the girl on the mountain. A sign? Filippo wonders whether he's missed something. Cristina had said, '*I've lived alone in this huge apartment ... since Giorgio, my partner left ... my phone number's on the kitchen table...*' Was that a come-on? Not sure. Did he have any other options? No. Besides, to exist in Cristina's eyes, revenge ... So, he'll have to try his luck. Tomorrow, he'll buy a nice cardboard cover, write on it 'ESCAPE, a story by Filippo Zuliani', slip the pages inside and put the whole thing in Cristina Pirozzi's letter-box, without a word of explanation. He wouldn't know what to say.

CHAPTER FOUR

FEBRUARY–MARCH 1988, PARIS

3 February

Filippo is wearing a clean white shirt when he walks into the bar, his breath tight, his mind numb. Yesterday, Cristina slid a note under his door. 'Meet me tomorrow, 7.30 p.m. at the Café Pouchkine, the Russian bar two streets away. We'll be able to have a quiet chat about your manuscript.' He has been in a semi-comatose state of waiting ever since, feeling as though he has stopped breathing. The interior is very dark; he blinks, hesitates, spots a shape waving at him from the back of the room and makes his way over. Cristina is sitting at a table, a glass of lager in front of her.

'Have a seat. Same?'

'No, I'll have a coffee.'

'Bad idea, the coffee's dreadful here.' She signals to the barman, then leans towards him, amused and curious.

'So tell me, this story, is it your story?' Filippo feels himself blushing, and hangs his head.

'It's a story that I've written.'

'I understand. It's a novel. But the main character, Filippo, is that you? The same name, is that a coincidence? Filippo, head bowed, avoids her gaze for a while, then takes the plunge.

'I could change the name.'

'What about Carlo? I think I've identified him, he's a former Red Brigades leader, isn't he? Did you know him personally?'

'Yes, I knew him.' Filippo smiles. 'You could put it like that. I knew him well. I was in jail with him – we were cellmates for six months. He was my friend. We escaped together, and now he's dead.'

'Like in the novel?'

'Like in the novel.'

'Was he Lisa's boyfriend?'

'I don't know. He never talked to me about her.'

'Have you told Lisa that?'

'Yes ... I think she was angry with me because of that...'

'Understandably. When did you write all this?'

Filippo is taken aback by the question. The answer seems obvious.

'At night. I'm a night watchman, as you know, in a tower, right near here. There's not much to do – you have to stare at a wall of CCTV monitors and nothing ever happens. In eight months we haven't had more than a dozen incidents, none of them serious. I've been writing every night since I've had the job, and I finished a few days ago. I didn't know what to do with it, that's why...'

He clears his throat and looks up, meeting her eye at last. This is the decisive moment.

'I'm no expert, but I can tell you that I read your novel in one go. It's good, maybe very good.'

Cristina stops, watches him. He gets his breath back, like a deep-sea diver surfacing. He relaxes, glances around the room, takes in the panelling, the banquettes and the heavy wooden armchairs with red leather cushions. He is on the verge of smiling. He really is charming, this young man whom she had taken for an almost completely tongue-tied illiterate. Author of a rather dazzling novel, or a small-time crook trying to pull off a scam? We'll see. But a good-looking lad in any case, and touching. Cristina takes a sip of beer, finds it has a delicious slight aftertaste of adventure, a feeling that has been cruelly lacking since the departure of Giorgio, her partner, the brilliant journalist.

'In any case, your story deserves to be published.'

'I'd love that, but I don't know how to go about it.'

'I can help you. I've lived here in Paris for a long time, with a well-known Italian journalist. I'm very familiar with the world of the press, and publishing. If you let me have your manuscript, I can have it read and possibly find you a publisher.'

He wavers for a moment, and then: 'I'm so thrilled that I don't even know what to say.'

'Don't say anything. Drink your vile cup of coffee and leave it to me. I'll probably be in touch next week.'

20 February

Summoned by the publisher to whom Cristina had sent his manuscript, Filippo enters the ancient building in the heart of Paris's Left Bank, fear in his belly and a vague sense of guilt. A warm welcome from the boss's PA, a beautiful blonde soberly dressed in black.

'Monsieur Zuliani, we're expecting you. Would you like me to relieve you of your jacket?'

He jumps.

'My jacket? No, I'll hold on to it.' *They were expecting me…* He wants to run away. Drop the whole thing. Impossible. Obsessive image of Cristina leaning towards him, a smile on her lips, her perfume and her beery breath. 'This story is your story.' He can't let her down.

He forces himself to advance, putting one foot in front of the other, letting his mind go blank.

The boss of the publishing house is waiting for him in his office. When Filippo walks in, he rises and comes to greet him. A handsome man in his late fifties, tall and slim, with a magnificent mane of kempt white hair. He shows Filippo over to a deep armchair.

'A coffee? Béatrice, would you kindly bring us two coffees.'

Then he turns to Filippo, and speaks to him in Italian, with relative fluency.

'Well, my dear sir, Cristina Pirozzi, who is a good friend

of mine, showed me your manuscript.' A pause, Filippo says nothing. 'Would you like to talk to me about it?' Filippo hasn't prepared anything, doesn't know what to say, he can't even remember what he's written in that wretched manuscript. His mind a blank, he stammers: 'No, I'd rather not ... I can't.'

The publisher raises his eyebrows, intrigued, but says nothing. The coffees arrive. They each take their cup, and Filippo becomes engrossed in watching the bubbles burst slowly on the surface of the coffee, with a sense of having ruined everything. The publisher gulps his coffee down, puts his cup back on the saucer and stares at Filippo belligerently.

'Right, we're interested in this story. But I'm going to be brutal, forgive me. If we work together, there has to be trust. Are you the author of this story? I mean are you the only author?'

Filippo is flabbergasted. He puts down his cup, looks up and finally dares meet the publisher's eye. On this territory, he is sure of himself, he becomes articulate, almost loquacious.

'Before going to jail, I'd never left Rome. My family, all my friends are there, and since my escape, all my ties have been broken. I'm alone in Paris, I don't know anyone. I've spent almost a year without talking to a soul. I wrote at night, every night. Without my realising it, without my deciding it, writing became my only lifeline. Who could have written it for me, and why, for what purpose?'

'Cristina?'

Filippo smiles.

'Cristina Pirozzi put me up when I was completely broke and had no job, she helped me survive, and I'm very grateful to her, but the first time she spoke to me was when I gave her my manuscript.'

The publisher knows Cristina. Credible, very credible, what the young man is saying. Obvious even. Judiciously observed. And his passion is convincing. The opposite of what he had feared initially; in fact, it was la Pirozzi who was trying to get herself back into the saddle with the help of this young man. He is won over, and proffers his hand to Filippo, who shakes it after a slight hesitation.

'Let's say no more about it, but you know the publishing world is full of surprises … Right, let's talk business. Your manuscript. We are agreed that it is definitely a novel. Let me make it plain: I don't want to know any more. I want to be able to carry on thinking and saying that it's a novel with total conviction. Are we agreed?'

'Yes. It's a novel.'

'Excellent. What we like about this novel is the authenticity of the voice, the true-to-life experience on every page, and I'm convinced the critics will feel the same way. Some passages are particularly outstanding from that point of view. Like the section where you describe the different attitudes of Carlo and the narrator towards guns, flying in the face of all the clichés. Carlo, with his political background, is very familiar with them, he loves them, looks at them, caresses them, while the narrator, who is a petty criminal, is afraid of them and, at some points, even goes so far as to dismiss their existence. Wonderful, given the ending, but you skate over this relationship to guns a bit too quickly. You'll need to go back to it, pad it out with action, dialogue, one or two anecdotes. Do you see what I mean?'

'Yes, I see.'

'Same for the affair between Carlo and Luciana. Nice touch to describe Filippo's love for Carlo through the way he observes relations between the two lovers.'

Filippo gulps.

'I didn't write that Carlo and Filippo were in love with one another…'

'Of course not, you couldn't have written it so blatantly – it's a feeling that neither of your characters can acknowledge. What you have done is much better. You can feel the emotion between them whenever they are in one another's presence, and it's excellent the way it is. You have written a novel about masculine friendship, a very particular form of love. I'm simply asking you to flesh out the scenes with the three of them – Luciana, Carlo and Filippo – in the same vein, if you feel you can.'

'Yes, I can.'

The publisher seems satisfied. He picks up the telephone.

'Béatrice, bring me the contracts. He turns to Filippo: 'We have found you a very good translator. He loves your book, and he'll help you to fine-tune it. I've discussed it with him, and he and I have the same approach. I think you'll get on very well together, he's charming. Oh, one thing, we've talked to our lawyers, and they recommend changing the first names and surnames, as well as the dates and place of the bank raid. As a precaution. The robbery that turned into a bloodbath and the violent death of Carlo Fedeli, whom you knew very well in fact, are too close in time, barely a year between them. You don't object? It *is* a novel, isn't it?'

Filippo leaves the publishing house in a daze. He pauses for a moment on the pavement outside and sees everything in a blur, the passers-by, the cars, despite the cold light of the bright winter sun. He sets off down the street and a cyclist knocks into him, swearing. That brings him to his senses. Telephone Cristina. He goes in search of a phone. Public telephone, the number of the occupational health centre at La Défense. Lisa answers. He recognises her voice, her Italian accent. Stuttering, he asks to speak to Dr Cristina Pirozzi. Lisa pauses briefly. Has she recognised him? He panics, then she puts him through, without a word. He breathes a sigh of relief.

'Cristina, it's done.' In his excitement, he can't get the words out fast enough. 'I've signed a contract. The book's coming out in May. I'm meeting the translator tomorrow to start polishing the text.' He gets his breath back. 'I wanted to thank you, sincerely. Without you…'

'No, Filippo, don't thank me. The publisher was swayed by your talent, not me. Look, I've got to see a patient now. Let's meet this evening at 7.30 at the Café Pouchkine. You can tell me all about it then. I want to know everything, and we'll celebrate your good news. All right?'

Filippo hangs up. *My talent.* He savours the words, letting them roll around his mouth. This evening at the Café Pouchkine. The stunning Cristina. The dream machine goes into gear.

He arrives at the Café Pouchkine early and heads for the back of the room, towards the same table as last time, and sits where she had sat, his eyes riveted on the door. In his head, jumbled thoughts, the thrill of success, *my book's going to be published*, and apprehension about the coming encounter. He is no longer the lost kid who slipped a manuscript into Cristina's letter box only two or three weeks ago. He is already a writer, but how does a writer behave? He has no idea how to inhabit the role. He loves the idea the publisher hinted at, that Cristina and he could have written the book together. It sets his mind to building a whole new world that belongs to just the two of them. They work in the same cramped room, seated facing one another on either side of a desk that fills almost the entire space, in an apartment that must belong to her, but which he can't see clearly yet. They swap pages covered in corrections, their hands brushing, their eyes meeting, a comment from time to time, the smell of her hair. He loves these moments of intimacy, just the two of them, like the ones he experienced with Carlo in their poky cell. But it is a dream. He shivers with the almost painful desire to exist in Cristina's eyes, re-lives the moment he first met her, one of the secret reasons, perhaps the most powerful one, that had spurred him to write in the first place, which seems completely beside the point. He can admit now, perhaps, at last. He repeats over and over, *I'm a writer. I wrote the book to make her look at me. She will look at me. One day, I'll win her, she'll be mine.* But he can't bring himself to believe it completely, to imagine how they will get together, the first moves, a seduction strategy. He doesn't order a drink, but sits absolutely still, devoting himself to waiting, relishing it, straining towards the woman who will soon be joining him.

When she arrives, her elegant form silhouetted against the street lights, she waves to him. His stomach is in knots. She walks towards him in the half light, wearing a loose-fitting camelhair coat, open to reveal a little tight-waisted dark brown suit jacket, a white blouse, full breasts – he can't breathe. She sits down, raises her arms, adjusts two wooden slides holding the mass of her copper hair in a chignon and lets her hair down. Attractive. She is aware of it, she uses it, she knows what she is doing. He doesn't want to be seduced, he wants to be the seducer, the conqueror. He is worried. Background music, the Gilbert Bécaud song:

Il avait un joli nom mon guide,
Nathalie…

She sings along.

Je pensais déjà
qu'après le tombeau de Lénine,
on irait au café Pouchkine,
boire un chocolat…

My guide had a pretty name,
Nathalie…
I was already thinking
That after Lenin's tomb,
We'd go to the Pushkin café
And drink hot chocolate…

She smiles at him.

'I adore the owner of this bar. He's a Russian with a great booming voice who worked as a tourist guide in Moscow for years. And at the end of each tour, people would always ask him if they could go for hot chocolate at the Café Pouchkine, which only exists in Bécaud's song. There's no such café in Moscow. He got fed up and found a way to get out of Russia and come here. He opened this Café Pouchkine, which the French dreamed of, here in Paris. Now, it's a haunt of the white Russians. It's a lovely story, isn't it? For a novelist ... Because you are a novelist, now.'

She laughs, and changes the subject. She's clearly in a talkative mood.

'What shall we drink, my friend? Chocolate isn't suitable for the occasion. Champagne here is a bit risky. I'll have a vodka, what about you?'

Furious with himself, he stammers, 'Same.'

She motions to the barman then turns back to him.

'Right, now tell me. I want to know everything. How did it go?'

'Very well, easy, fast. He gave me a coffee, the contracts were ready to be signed. I was expecting something different, more of a conflict. Some sort of battle.'

'You said the book's coming out in May. That's very quick, but not a very good time of year. September, when all the major books are published would have been better. What's the initial print run?'

'I don't know.'

'It's in the contract.'

'I haven't read it.'

'You signed without reading it?'

'There were a lot of pages. If I'd read it, I wouldn't have understood anything.' He is embarrassed. 'And I was so overwhelmed that I couldn't read.'

Inwardly he chides himself for parading his naivety and vulnerability in front of this woman who is so sure of herself and so seductive. The barman brings the vodkas, giving him the chance to collect himself. As they clink glasses, she gazes at him with new eyes. A smooth face with a strong bone structure. Pale complexion, a well-defined mouth, a mass of black hair, dark brown eyes. A youthful, offbeat look. He, a small-time crook whose fate had led him to flirting with guns, terrorism, death and now writing. And still clueless. Frankly attractive, why not admit it to herself? Now he has entered her world, a world he knows nothing about. He needs to be initiated, protected, and she knows she can do that. She even wants to. She might feel less alone, and life would be more fun. Mentor, Pygmalion, hundreds of references, a wonderful role. An opportunity for the taking.

Filippo, ill at ease under her gaze, lowers his eyes, takes a sip, tries to take back the initiative: 'The thing the publisher wanted to know was whether I'd written the book myself, all by myself. He seemed to have doubts...'

'Doubts? But I promised him you had.'

Filippo jumps.

'Promised ... but how can you be so certain. You don't know me.'

Cristina leans towards him laughing, perfectly relaxed.

'Do you imagine, young man, that I would have given a publisher friend a manuscript handed to me by a virtual stranger without being able to vouch for its authenticity, at the risk of damaging my own credibility? I found an excuse to ask Antoine, your work colleague, to come to my clinic for an occupational health check-up. We chatted, and he told me how you spent your nights writing.'

A pause.

'Come on, relax.' She places her hand over his, a soothing gesture of familiarity. 'I'm delighted to say, I found your colleague entirely convincing.'

Filippo turns pale, bows his head and feels his heart contract in his breast. Cristina's touch makes him burn, he moves his hand away sharply, and toys with his glass. The vodka is setting his guts on fire. This woman ... His desire evaporates. The memory of what had happened in the mountains assaults him, clouds his vision. He had felt the same pang deep in his heart when Carlo abandoned him (the cold, the miserable bag of provisions, total solitude), without then being able to understand the source of that pain. He had repressed it, tried not to think about it any more. A wasted effort, it is still there. But right now, in this café, he knows. Carlo talked of *his* escape. He had told him: *We part company here.* He alone made the decisions. Whether or not he'd said that to protect Filippo, it made no difference. The man who had enthralled him with descriptions of meetings where each person's view was taken into account and arose from a collective consciousness, the outbursts of violence and the elation of the anonymous and leaderless crowd that had given him so much to dream about – that man had no right to decide his fate for him and without him. That was his betrayal. Filippo now knows that in writing about the escape, he has created a Carlo faithful to himself, more real, a Carlo he could legitimately love. And now, this woman he is determined to vanquish is behaving like the Carlo of the past. *Young man ... vouch for its authenticity ... not damage my credibility ... I asked your colleague, Antoine, to come to my clinic...* In her hands, he is a thing, and she had taken the liberty of inquiring about him behind his back. She still sees him as a lost kid; she talked about his past whereas he dreamed of cavalcades, invasions and victories.

Don't get sucked in. Danger. She'll destroy me, she'll devour me. I know what I don't want, but I don't know how to get what I do want. Get out. Now. Run. Save my skin. Think later.

Filippo rises to his feet, his face inscrutable. He stammers: 'Sorry, it's late, I'm working tonight, I have to go.'

And he leaves her sitting there, dumbfounded, in front of the two vodkas that have barely been touched. In the background, Bécaud has given way to a double-bass duo.

It takes Cristina a few seconds to realise that Filippo has walked out, for good. Incredulity. She downs her vodka in one, to clear her mind and to try and regain her footing. *I've just done him a huge favour, which he seemed to appreciate. Rude, really, very rude. Not surprising. Lout. No, not rude, ungrateful, that's worse. Now he's got what he wants, he dumps me.*

Then, without seeing it coming, she is hit by a wave of despair. In her forties, loneliness. For ever? A life sentence? She drinks the vodka that Filippo barely touched.

I played the seductress, almost out of habit, and it didn't work. I have to face facts, I'm no longer an attractive woman. What do I have left? A job that bores me…

She signals to the barman: another.

What was I expecting this evening? Hard to say, I don't know. Romance, a young man to pamper, life, action, perhaps even a lover. An end to my loneliness. In any case, he owes me something.

She mulls over the evening to try and pinpoint the moment it had all gone wrong.

Arrival, Bécaud, he'd laughed, his account of the meeting with the publisher, so far so good. The publisher's doubts as to whether Filippo could be the author of the book. But she had had no doubts, and told him so. No problem. And she placed her hand over his. Skin to skin. That was when everything fell apart. Filippo was profoundly disturbed. He lowered his head and jerked his hand away quite violently. And he departed. A doubt surfaces. So young, good-looking, prison, that passionate relationship with Carlo… *He's gay. Just my luck.*

The barman brings her third vodka.

CHAPTER FIVE

MAY 1988

Paris, 10 May

L'Univers des Livres, review by Jeanne Champaud
A few days ago, the publisher of *Escape*, the novel by Filippo
Zuliani that will be appearing in bookshops this week, gave
me a copy of the proofs saying, 'Read these. I think you'll
be surprised.' I was. And I'm prepared to bet that I won't be
the only one, and that we'll be hearing about this novel when
the literary prize season is upon us this autumn.

On first reading, this novel appears to tell a story that is
not particularly original: a young hoodlum and a veteran terrorist, a survivor of the 'Years of Lead', meet by chance in
prison and break out together. Then, as much out of choice
as of necessity, they team up and organise a bank heist that
turns into a bloodbath. The formula seems to be that of the
traditional crime novel, but appearances can be deceptive.
This novel overturns all the rules of the genre; it is a lot more
and a lot better than a simple story of small-time crooks.
The book has two plots that are inextricably interwoven,
ultimately merging.

The sub-plot is that of the two protagonists' escape from
jail, the preparation of the heist, the heist itself and the
resulting fiasco, against a background of gangland turf wars.
It is the simple, effective storyline that hooks the reader
from beginning to end, without allowing a pause for breath.
Grafted on to that is the 'main' story, the one that the veteran

terrorist tells his young companion, initially in prison, in the form of flashbacks, then during the run-up to the bank robbery. What the book reveals is both how the Italian left-wing extremist groups, born out of the widespread workers' struggles of the 1970s, very quickly turned to violence and ended in gangsterism in the '80s, and the extent to which that violence, perhaps because of its radical nature, was able to seduce our young hoodlum, and probably many other young Italians, to the point of binding him to his cellmate until death. When they are on the run, their shared love of violence inevitably leads to serious crime, into which the young hoodlum introduces his companion, then follows him, in a sort of mirror initiation novel. A classic path for an entire lost generation.

The narrative is raw, full of suspense, emotions, told with tremendous honesty. No caricatures, no stereotypes, the characters are all wonderfully alive. And the author has a definite, well-controlled sense of dramatic tension.

When I discovered that this is a debut novel by a very young Italian, who has been a refugee in France for the past few months, I naturally wanted to meet him to find out how much of this story was autobiographical, and how such a young man could have written something so accomplished.

We met in fairly conventional surroundings, near the publishing house, in the bar of a big Paris hotel with deep leather armchairs, coffee tables and a secluded atmosphere. The author arrived with an interpreter and the publisher's publicist: they are keeping a close eye on their little prodigy. It soon turned out that we didn't need the interpreter, since with a bit of effort we managed to understand one another. He is indeed very young, barely twenty-three, I'm told, but looks eighteen – a delicate figure, with the appearance of a teenage pop idol beneath a mop of black hair. He sits bolt upright, slightly rigid, self-conscious, in his blue jeans and white T-shirt. He rarely smiles and speaks very little. I could feel he was on the defensive, which is a very appealing admission of vulnerability. I tell him right away that I'm enchanted.

We get off to a rocky start. When I ask him how much of the book is autobiographical, he snaps back, 'It's a novel. That's it.' I press him a little, mentioning what I've read in the author biography provided by his publisher, plus my own research into his past life of crime, his spell in prison, his escape, the similarities between the episodes in his novel and recent events in Italy, and in which he himself was involved, directly or indirectly – that is for him to say. And lastly, I ask him about applying for political asylum in France, which he has apparently been given, or will be given shortly. That is certainly not an award for picking tourists' pockets on the streets of Rome. If I want answers to those questions, he replies, I can talk to his lawyer, who is also the publisher's lawyer.

So it's back to talking about literature, nothing but literature. Very well. I get straight to the point. Given that he spent his youth in the streets and prisons of Rome, where did he learn to write in a language that is so simple, so effective and sometimes so moving? Was it in books, and if so, which ones? Which authors have influenced him? That earns me a wan smile.

In his family home, there were no books, so he didn't read any, and still today, the sight of a well-stocked bookcase makes him feel anxious. He learned to write in prison, not in books. Learned to listen, first of all, he says, to listen to the political prisoners talking about their hopes, their exploits, their defeats. Learned also to love the language those men spoke, which was magnificent because it was resonant with passion and despair, and that is what made it absolutely fascinating. As a result of listening, he absorbed their way of telling a story. He thought about all those prisoners when he began to write. And it was easy. He insists, 'The words came all by themselves.' But why write? At this, Filippo Zuliani becomes animated, drops his aloof air. 'Why? To allow those people an existence, a life.' He hesitates, then continues, 'And also to understand my own life. Maybe above all. Literature is life, isn't it? Isn't that what you often say in your articles?'

Life? His life? I won't be any the wiser. He seems to be steering the entire conversation to focus only on literature, on the novel, and to divert attention from his own experience. It is hard to imagine that a book that draws so heavily on current affairs and has such richness is not inspired by real life. Filippo Zuliani won't say, but... The main thing is that Filippo Zuliani has written a real 'American-style' novel, sweeping in scope, inspired by a chaotic existence, and as hard-hitting as a punch in the stomach. A must-read.

16 May

The publication of *Escape* and the reviews in the French press make the Italian refugees anxious and angry. The Sunday afternoon meeting is likely to be crowded and difficult for Lisa, thinks Roberto. Reviving the pain, the wrench and the shock of Carlo's death a year on, when the wounds are still raw ... she is strong. Perhaps this will be the opportunity for her to reach closure, but he doubts it. He drops by to see her in the morning, with a selection of Sicilian pastries. Lisa is lounging around, demoralised.

'This novel breaks my heart.'

'I'm sure.'

'The character who everyone calls Carlo isn't the man I knew and loved. A man of passion, of conviction, a poet. Portrayed as a gang boss. He never took part in armed action. I did, you know I did, Roberto, with all that implies. I'm paying for it, I don't ever want to talk about it again. But not him.'

'Lisa, I know what you're going through and I'm here.'

'He's assassinating Carlo a second time. A public execution. I wasn't expecting it. Nobody had the foresight to warn me. When I found out that Cristina had put Filippo in touch with the publisher, without having the decency to say anything to me, I decided never to speak to her again, which doesn't make life easy at work, as you can imagine.'

'We're going to talk about the novel at the meeting this afternoon.'

'Without me.'

'You have to come.'

'No way. Last year, when I wanted to try and find out how Carlo had been assassinated, I asked for their help. Nobody lifted a finger, Giovanni told everyone I was paranoid, and no one has been in touch with me since then. I'm not prepared to forget that. And I've made no headway in my investigation into his death.'

'This book is going to have political repercussions – we should all discuss it together.'

'Political repercussions! Are you kidding? What political repercussions? Since Carlo's death, everything we feared, like everything we wanted to avoid, has happened in spades. The Red Brigades' declaration was buried deep, it was never discussed or commented on by anyone. The left's programme is the same as that of the right. First goal: massive repression of the far left, thousands of activists in prison, five thousand according to my figures, no amnesty, those turned informant, the traitors, held up as a pillar of justice and model citizens. And a new Law of Dissociation, a brilliant invention, that has hit us hard. Second goal: clear the assassins involved in the wholesale massacres, the secret service henchmen. In less than a year, they've had the effrontery to clear the Piazza Fontana killers, the Brescia and the *Italicus* train bombers. And no one protests. So they'll continue. Result: some of our former activists, completely disoriented, can't stop the violence. Two more supposedly political assassinations this month, for which there is no justification now that the war is over. From that point of view, you were right: setting up Carlo was pointless, we're big enough to commit suicide all by ourselves.'

'I'm glad to hear you say so.'

'And the rot is contagious. As a result of being afraid to take us back, the Italian Communist Party is on its last legs, taking with it an entire shared political culture. People don't do politics any more in Italy, they do business, it's the grand ball of the corruptors and the corrupt.'

She stands up, opens her arms and smiles at Roberto.

'May I have this dance?'

'Stop, you're doing my head in. We know all that. Sit down and listen to me. I'm talking about the impact that this book might have here, in France. The papers say that Zuliani has applied for political asylum. If he gets it, he'll be giving the Italian government the perfect excuse to ask the French to abolish political refugee status. You, me, lots of others, we'll all end our lives in jail.'

Lisa eats a pastry in silence staring out at the garden, and Roberto doesn't rush her. Then he adds, 'The lawyers will be there. Their opinion is decisive.'

A fresh silence, then Lisa:

'You win, Roberto, as always.'

The vast, drab room where the meeting is taking place is packed. The discussion has not yet begun. People crowd round the copious buffet and the noise level is deafening. Lisa steps into the room, tense, as if she wishes she were elsewhere. Giovanni is sitting on a table right beside the door, legs dangling, glass in hand, talking and laughing loudly.

'Carlo's double, betrayed and assassinated by his accomplices in a spectacular coup, I'm sure Lisa appreciates that. Conspiracy theory and showmanship, it's all there. She could almost have penned the scenario herself.'

Lisa plants herself in front of him and hisses:

'You'll say anything to sound clever.'

'And you love making an entrance. We're quits, dear Lisa.'

Those close to both Giovanni and Lisa start telling others

about the heated exchange. Roberto senses a row brewing and hastily calls for silence, then opens the meeting.

'We're gathered here today with our lawyers to discuss Zuliani's book and its potential repercussions.' People turn towards Lisa who says simply: 'The book is a novel. Like all novels, it is of no importance, now let's change the subject.'

While one of the lawyers explains that things aren't quite like that, and that Zuliani, his publisher and the press are making the most of the ambiguous relations the author is alleged to have had with one of the Red Brigades leaders, Giovanni, sitting next to Lisa, leans over to her and whispers: 'We robbed banks a few years ago, and better than Carlo. I remember a period when we were doing one a month. Nobody made such a fuss back then.'

Lisa replies in an undertone: 'But those were different times. That's politics for you, comrade.'

Concluding his speech, the lawyer also turns to Lisa: 'Can you tell us what makes you so sure that this novel is entirely a work of fiction? It is important in determining how we are to proceed.'

'Because I have learned it from two different sources. Carlo telephoned me straight after his escape. Don't look so sceptical, Giovanni. I already told you a year ago, and I'm happy to be more specific today. When I was on a clandestine assignment in Paris, we used to have a regular telephone appointment. As soon as I read about his escape in the papers, my first reflex was to reactivate the appointment. And he called.'

She leans over to Giovanni:

'I don't need to tell you anything further. Satisfied? Or do you want me to tell you the place and times of our appointments too?'

Giovanni gives a dismissive wave to indicate 'fair enough.' Lisa goes on: 'Carlo told me about the Red Brigades' open letter that had just been published, about his escape – which he described as a final embodiment of "practising the objective", the policy adopted by the movement in the autumn of '69. In other words, highly political language. He hadn't become a gangster. I was concerned about the young hoodlum who broke out with him. I thought he could be a potential threat, and said so. Carlo assured me that they had already parted company.'

Lisa speaks in a strangled voice. Even after all this time, she cannot get used to it. She coughs and continues: 'Then, this Filippo Zuliani turned up on my doorstep, a few days after Carlo's death. That too, I told you about at the time. He told me how he and Carlo had gone their separate ways immediately after the escape, which corroborated what Carlo had told me. He told me that Carlo had arranged to meet up with him in Milan, a month later. Whether it's true or not doesn't matter. In any case, Zuliani began to make his way northwards. He walked for three weeks in the mountains, without meeting a soul. When he arrived in Bologna, he read the newspapers and learned about the bank raid and Carlo's death. And that was what frightened him, the idea that he might be suspected of being Carlo's accomplice – understandably, since he was unable to provide an alibi. It was a knee-jerk reaction, he seemed lost, and I had the feeling that at that point, he was telling the truth. And I still think so. As far as I'm concerned, the book is definitely a novel, constructed from reading certain newspaper articles that bear no relation to the facts.'

Chiara has slipped in beside Roberto and some of the lawyers. She speaks with fieriness and resentment.

'This business has done a lot of damage, both here and back in Italy, to those of us who aren't gangsters. Just read the papers, you'll see. It's sickening, they're all banging on about "The Italian left-wing extremists' deadly and unstoppable slide into crime". That tars us with the same brush. And unfortunately, I'm not certain that the book is purely fictitious, as you claim. I knew Carlo well too...'

Lisa bristles, Roberto quakes. *No, not that...*

'…and I think that this Zuliani knew him well, from the way he describes Carlo's love of guns, girls and showing off. The warmth of their relationship makes his account credible.'

Lisa straightens herself up, she has lost her cool and her voice becomes shrill.

'Love of guns … Carlo… you're crazy, Chiara. You talk as though we were all gunslingers. None of us loved firearms. I know what I'm talking about. And even if Carlo agreed with the Red Brigades' military actions, he himself never touched a gun. I'm saying it here, for all those who didn't know us, and now that it's all over: Carlo was in charge of logistics for the Red Brigades' underground operators – organising accommodation, transport, allocating funds. He took the same risks as all of us, but the organisation was cellular, he was never involved in any armed operation. This whole story is outrageous.'

'What about the women, Lisa… ?'

Roberto leaps up.

'That's enough, Chiara. Stop that now. Let's get back to the topic of our meeting.' He turns to the lawyers. 'Does Zuliani have a chance of obtaining political asylum, and what should we do?'

'We have met Filippo Zuliani once – Lisa sent him to us last year, on his arrival in Paris. We found him fairly insipid, and we didn't pay much attention to him. That was clearly a mistake. He has a lawyer, who has not been in contact, so we have no direct knowledge of his application. But we think he has a chance, yes. Refugee status is awarded arbitrarily, at the discretion of the powers that be. And since the president prides himself on being a man of letters, anything is possible. Especially since the book is good and is getting excellent reviews. His publisher is supporting him and it will probably sell well. To defuse things, we'll put the word out via our networks, repeat what Lisa has told us, explain that Zuliani only had a very distant connection to Carlo, and that his book is a novel. Lisa, have you got any concrete evidence you can give us?'

Lisa closes her eyes, grits her teeth and swallows her irritation.

'No.'

'It would be ideal if you could come up with something.'

'I'm prepared to work at it, energetically too. Last year, I asked for help, but no one came forward. Will it be any different this time?'

'Of course we're prepared to help you, all of us here, we French lawyers as well as you Italians. Meanwhile, I advise everyone to be very careful in public. No comment without consulting us first. And let's hope that no one will be talking about the book after the summer.'

May

After the publication of Jeanne Champaud's piece in the *Univers des Livres*, the publisher is inundated with requests from various newspapers and magazines for interviews with Filippo Zuliani, many more than anticipated. Discussion between the publisher and the publicist. How much should they focus on the breakout, should they go all-out or softly-softly? The publisher is not sure. He fears that Filippo might not be able to cope with all the media attention and will cause a scandal by taking credit for the assassinations, for example. The publicist, on the other hand, feels that the book is going to be big, so it is unthinkable not to use it, and she is confident she can handle the young Italian bad boy. When several radio stations and a TV channel request interviews, the publicist is proved right. She asks Filippo to come in for a brief 'meeting to arrange his schedule'. He arrives, his heart pounding. Conflicting feelings. The publishing house could be the family he dreams of, he wants to feel at home here, but somehow can't. He is afraid of letting everyone down, and admits to himself that he is ready to do anything so as not to be thrown out, which he feels puts him in a position of weakness. Besides, ready to do anything ... Would that be enough?

The publicist, Adèle, sees him in her office, a cramped, very cluttered room, with a French window opening on to a well-kept garden. She smiles at him, invites him to sit in a huge, old armchair, and offers him a coffee.

'You seem tense. Relax, it's all good news. There's quite a buzz around *Escape*. She opens a file and reads out the requests she has received, commenting on each one.

'There's a terrific word-of-mouth effect, no doubt about it, and that's very valuable because it's not something you can create, but when there is one, you can build on it and consolidate it. Do you see?'

'No. Not really.'

'Never mind. That's my job, trust me. First we need to try and understand what fires the critics' interest. And the public's, if it takes off as we're hoping it will…'

She gazes at Filippo who sits very still, staring fixedly, fighting back the waves of anxiety.

'…in addition to the book's literary merit, of course. But if you knew how many good books never find an audience … in the case of *Escape,* the thing they're all talking about is the thrill the journalists get from rubbing shoulders with a criminal, who may be a cop-killer. A type they rarely get to meet.'

Filippo is ashen, he feels a mounting panic. He stares at the floor. Adèle continues, undaunted: 'Let me be clear. If you're possibly a cop-killer, that makes you an attractive young hoodlum. But if you are a declared cop-killer and proud of it, then you become a criminal no one wants to be associated with. It's a delicate balance. We have to maintain the ambiguity without putting you directly in danger. "It's a novel, talk to my lawyer," as we agreed, and as you did with Champaud, right? But only as a last resort. Beforehand, make a few concessions, tantalise these good people's imaginations. You can admit that you escaped from prison with Carlo Fedeli, a former Red Brigades member who was killed a little later in a bank robbery. In any case, people will find out – it's already public knowledge. You admit his death affected you, and it sparked the idea. Add that all literary fiction includes elements of real life, and stop there. Say any more and it becomes dangerous. Steer the conversation back to the novel and repeat "lawyer". Are you with me? Agreed?'

'Yes.'

'Second thing, and just as important, the character of the author himself.'

Filippo jumps, leans towards her, his mouth open to protest. She raises her hand to stop him.

'Don't panic, I know what I'm doing, leave it to me. When a book arrives in my hands, it's done, I have no power over the product. But the author … Here I think we really have to milk the distinction. Surprise them. The average literary critic imagines that a hoodlum will be violent and unkempt. So be very calm, say little, as you did with Champaud, that was perfect. If you do find yourself under attack – and that's bound to happen – you need to be prepared. No argument, whatever you do, don't try and have the last word, or be smart, but answer slightly off the point using carefully measured words, even a cliché, and put on the meaningful expression of someone who's not revealing all he knows. Let the interviewer be the only one who's aggressive and clever. I'll be there, look at me and I'll signal to you, that'll help you. And now your dress. Nothing scruffy, obviously. Avoid jeans, T-shirts and trainers. A slightly over-studied elegance. Well-cut cotton trousers, jackets, or long-sleeved shirts, excellent colour coordination. Leather English shoes. I'll give you the addresses of some good shops. Any questions?'

'No.'

His voice falters. Filippo isn't sure he will be able to achieve the many goals she has set him, but he keeps his anxiety to himself.

'One more thing, and then we'll be done. Do you intend to leave your job as a security guard?'

'No,' he retorts at once, clearly and without hesitation
'Why not?'
A pause.
'Because.'
Silence. Adèle waits for him to elaborate, which he doesn't.
She goes on: 'OK. As you wish. When journalists ask you that,
which they probably will, just add a few comments about
night work stimulating your imagination. You're a writer now,
don't forget.'
Filippo sits hunched in his chair, not moving a muscle.
'Right. Shall we move on to your diary now?'

A routine sets in. Filippo feels as if he's virtually under house
arrest at his publisher's, under the watchful eye of the publicist, and it suits him perfectly. Super-professional, as always,
Adèle dissects Paris literary life bit by bit, like unlocking
drawers, then giving him the keys. She sets him very clear,
very precise rules of behaviour, what he should and shouldn't
say, and how to say it. He applies them unquestioningly, glad
to find a ready-made existence. And it works. His press interviews take place in a little lounge at the publisher's, just next
to the boss's office. Before each appointment, Adèle inspects
him carefully in front of the big mirror in the toilet, checking
each detail of his outfit, commenting on and correcting any
mistakes. But there are fewer and fewer. When someone takes
the trouble to explain things, Filippo learns fast. On this occasion, he is wearing a dark-brown suit and pink shirt, which he
dons as readily as others put on blue overalls to go to work in
a factory. At home, he has practised walking, sitting down and
inhabiting his new clothes until it feels like second nature, as if
he has always dressed like this. Then he unexpectedly catches
his reflection in the mirrors in the lift, on his way out. After his
initial surprise, he contemplates the man looking back at him
with incredulity, and a hint of envy.
In his conversations with the journalists, he quickly finds

his bearings – the restrictions on what he can or must say have been carefully signposted by the publicist, and he happily keeps to them. She sits in on all the interviews, always in the background, and he soon learns to read from her face whether to steam ahead, veer off or back-pedal. Her presence gives him confidence.

As anticipated, the journalists have done their homework, asking specific questions about his escape with Carlo Fedeli, who died three weeks later during a bank robbery that was strikingly similar to the one in the novel. So how much of the book is autobiographical?

A glance towards the publicist.

'Yes, I was in prison and there I met Carlo Fedeli who became a very good friend of mine. He used to speak eagerly and eloquently about Italy's recent history, especially about those years dubbed the "Years of Lead" by the press, and which Carlo, if I remember correctly, called "the years of fire". I used to listen to him for hours, not having lived through anything like it myself. I have him to thank for inspiring me to write, and for my style in doing so.'

The journalists would push him, asking for more precise details.

'You broke out of prison with Carlo Fedeli, as everyone knows. Is it your escape that you write about in your novel? Did you take part in the robbery during which Carlo Fedeli was shot dead? How much of the account is fictitious?'

Filippo puts on a masterful show of being annoyed.

'Yes, Carlo Fedeli's death and the circumstances in which it occurred affected me deeply. But why are you asking me these questions? My escape? The hold-up? What do you want to know? You'll have noticed that the novel isn't written in the first person. I've done my job as a novelist, that's all. Obviously, in my writing I draw on the "events" of my life, like my escape, but I have nothing further to tell you. Do you ask other novelists the same questions? All novelists' imaginations are inspired by real-life events. There is an autobiographical element in my novel, as in all novels. No more, no less.'

The publicist smiles.

'Any other questions? My current job? Night watchman. No, I don't read when I'm on duty. I didn't read in prison, I listened and now, at night, I don't read, I write. In prison, I heard stories, complaints, flights of fancy, fragments of broken stories. The transition to writing wasn't easy. We can talk about that, if you like, about the process of writing rather than my life story.'

At this point, the interview abruptly ends. As the publicist had warned him, writing is a subject that very few literary critics want to explore, over and above a few well-worn clichés and a handful of adjectives.

Adèle discreetly mimes her silent applause. He is happy and thanks her with a smile. He is grateful to this woman who never uses her female charms. She does her job. He is aware how much he owes her, although he does not feel in any way obligated to her.

First radio interview, flawless. The interviewer finds his Italian accent charming.

His first TV appearance is arranged. He turns out to be very telegenic. Make-up and lighting: without losing that pop idol look, his face is sharper, more forceful.

The publicist has organised a book signing in a major book-shop on Boulevard Saint-Germain. When she talks to him about it ('meet your readers'), he panics. He doesn't know anything about readers. Neither his family, nor his Rome gang, his fellow prisoners, his colleague at the Tour Albassur, nor he himself were readers. He had wanted to write for Lisa and Cristina, women he knew, and he'd had a very specific purpose. But readers?

'Will there be a lot of people?'

'I hope so. I'll do my utmost to ensure there are.'

He pictures himself surrounded by strangers calling him

a liar and an imposter, and proposes they avoid such a con-
frontation. But Adèle is adamant. It is a must and there is no
getting away from it.

Given her efficiency, the date and the venue of the signing
are announced in all the major newspapers and on some radio
stations. The book has garnered a great deal of critical attention and aroused people's curiosity, so there is a big turnout.

The bookshop's layout makes it difficult and slow to move
around. On the ground floor, the publisher has laid on a buffet
around which the regulars cluster, blocking access to the staircase and the mezzanine where the signing table is set up. Some
people are coming up, others going down, it is all a bit chaotic.
Small groups stand around, halfway up, deep in conversation, before jostling their way to the buffet. There is a sense of
success in such a crush of fans.

Sitting at a table in one corner of the mezzanine, Filippo
begins signing with a trembling hand, not daring to look up
from the flyleaves on which he scrawls his name. Adèle, sitting
behind him, is chatting with a friend. Before him, he is aware
of a wall of bodies all merged together; without looking up he
takes the proffered books and asks the person's name, signs,
hands the book back and takes the next. This task absorbs him
and gradually he relaxes. He is not conscious of any hostil-
ity in the atmosphere. He straightens up. He sees a moving
mass, mainly women, and just in front of him, leaning slightly
towards the table, clutching their books, two girls stand
smiling at him. They are blonde and fresh, and he finds them
beautiful. He feels flattered. One of them says: 'Thank you for
your book.'

He grows flustered. His shyness delights the reader, who
adds: 'You're just like your characters.'

The other girl continues: 'You write about the world of male
violence with sympathetic characters who appeal to women
like us.'

'Yes, we want to hug them.'

'You too, by the way.'

Giggles.

Filippo is at a loss, out of his depth. What are they talking about? His book? Impossible… He checks the title of the book in his hand. *Escape.* Oh yes they are, no question. On auto-pilot, he writes on the flyleaf, 'Thank you for being so beautiful', and signs. He watches them walk off, elbowing their way through the crowd, their books under their arms.

Adèle comes over to him, then whispers in his ear:

'Chatting up the girls, are we?' Filippo stutters. 'Don't panic, you're not the first.'

While he tries to think of an answer, the throng swells even more. It is becoming a hand-to-hand battle with a seething mass of bodies. He is inundated, thrilled, exhausted. An hour later, the crowd ebbs away, leaving him feeling faintly nauseous.

When the bookshop closes, Adèle kisses him – a new experience – and sends him home in a taxi. A hot bath, then he lies down, closes his eyes and pictures the crowd, hears it again, with its disjointed words and snatches of conversation. His first physical contact with his readers. Disorienting. A whole mass of readers. Readers who look at him, but he cannot recognise himself in their eyes. He feels as if he is living a thousand fragmented, atomised existences, outside his control. But it is his book, his signature. No doubt about that. Beleaguered by the flood of sensations, he gives up trying to order them. *I'll think about it all later.* And falls asleep.

By the end of May, Filippo Zuliani has become media savvy and is able to play the role of writer to perfection when faced with the press, readers, or booksellers. He has mastered every nuance, every inflection and become the darling of the Paris literary scene. A representative of the 'dangerous' classes, a 'raw artist' who's been tamed, a handsome young man with brown eyes. But deep down, without ever talking to anyone about it, he knows it is a made-up part, a usurper's role maybe, and doubt lurks inside him like a shadow. He is constantly anxious that his mind will go blank, or that he'll perform badly and disappoint. It is hugely stressful, but he carries it off. And that almost imperceptible little hint of underlying anxiety only adds to his charm.

Escape makes it into the week's top-ten bestseller list. It reaches tenth place in the first week, up to seventh the following week. The publisher is optimistic about the future – things have taken off fast, and should get even better. Filippo isn't informed of the sales figures, Adèle doesn't think it necessary, it might make their relations difficult if he gets big-headed. Better to wait till the trend is confirmed, and besides, he doesn't seem bothered for the time being, he never asks how well the book is selling.

Each afternoon, after the round of press interviews, Filippo goes back to his studio flat in Neuilly. He changes his clothes, eats a sandwich, drinks a coffee, and fantasises about Cristina. Impossible to stop thinking about her. She fills his mind the minute he stops performing in front of his audience. He is tormented by his inability to penetrate her world and by his aching wish to erase his frantic flight from the Café Pouchkine. He dreams of finding someone to hold his hand and tell him what to do down to the last detail, as Adèle does in his life as a writer, so that he can rewind their disastrous encounter and give it a different outcome. But there are no candidates for the job. Invent a future with Cristina? His imagination fails him. He cannot even replay the scene that has begun to take shape, the two of them sitting at the same desk, working together on the same text, a paradise lost. He feels nothing but empty longing. Every day, he veers between desire and the fear of running into her in the downstairs lobby or the apartment entrance, but he never does. Maybe she is avoiding him. Holding his breath, he listens out for movements, for sounds from her apartment, but there are few signs of life on the other side of the wall.

While waiting for something to happen that will kick-start his life back into motion, he occasionally (when he has the time and before going on to La Défense) makes a detour via the nearby Bois de Boulogne where love can be bought. Without shame and almost without desire, a basic hygienic procedure. An impoverished sex life without illusions, not so different from his practice in Rome, when his little gang ran a dozen or so completely lost girls, supplying them with dope, passing them around among themselves, and using them sometimes as bait to attract lonely tourists.

Then, at 10 p.m., he begins his second life. Security guard at the Tour Albassur. The corridors and offices are empty of their ghosts now that the book is finished, and he and Antoine have got into the habit of playing endless games of draughts. Here he unwinds, breathes freely, de-stresses, purges his anxiety, his mind empty and calm. A sort of intermission, an in-between time of blessed relaxation. One day, perhaps, he might feel like writing again. He has no idea whether or not he will, and there is no rush. For the time being, he tries not to think about it.

CHAPTER SIX

JUNE 1988, FRANCE–ITALY

10 June
La Repubblica publishes an opinion piece by Romano Sebastiani, one of the foremost public prosecutors of the Milan counter-terrorist section.

Two months ago to the day, our very dear friend Roberto Ruffili died. A renowned international constitutionalist, he was assassinated by the Red Brigades PCC, the notorious splinter group that emerged from the break-up of the murderous Red Brigades. It is clear that Italy is not finished with 'red' terrorism, and the tragic legacy of the Years of Lead. At this same moment the French literary establishment chooses to crown a young Italian writer, Filippo Zuliani and his novel *Escape,* with critical and commercial success. We might be delighted at the Paris intelligentsia's sudden interest in Italian culture, if this book did not pose a serious moral and political problem. Let's take a closer look.

  With considerable skill, the novel recounts a tragic event: two men break out of jail together, a former Red Brigades leader and a young Roman hoodlum. The two men linked by a close 'masculine friendship', decide to make their living by robbing banks. Devilishly romantic … but you don't become a bank robber overnight, and their first hold-up of a big Milan bank ends in disaster. The Red Brigades veteran is shot dead, and one of his accomplices assassinates a *carabiniere* and a security guard while making his getaway. A dubious tale, verging on a glorification of the criminals, but that is not the issue here. The novel's plot depicts precisely, down to the last detail, Carlo Fedeli's escape from his Rome prison in February 1987, and how the Red Brigades' former head of logistics turned gangster. It also describes the heist, based on that of the Piemonte-Sardegna bank in Milan three weeks later, during which Fedeli was shot dead, as reconstructed in the police investigation. Only the names of the characters, the date and place of the robbery have been changed. The moral problem, as I was saying, is that this is a shameless commercial exploitation of a very recent, and still unsolved criminal case, since the accomplices remain unidentified. It demonstrates no consideration for the victims' families, but there is worse to come.

The novel's author, Filippo Zuliani, is clearly the young hoodlum who broke out of jail with Carlo Fedeli. Could he also be the accomplice in the robbery, as the novel implies? If he has information on these events, and from reading his novel it would seem that he does, then Filippo Zuliani should return and disclose it before an Italian court, and not in a novel, in which he plays on every possible form of ambiguity.

The matter also presents a political problem, and a sizeable one. Just when things are so precarious here in Italy, President Mitterrand feels that France should offer asylum to certain Italian political refugees. That is his choice, not ours. But how can he justify the fact that this asylum extends to a petty crook, a criminal on the run, who, we are told, has apparently been granted refugee status as well? But perhaps our information is wrong, for we have received no official notification on this matter.

In any case, Filippo Zuliani's place, novelist or otherwise, is not in the salons of Paris. Instead it is plainly here in Italy, where he must come and face the courts over his escape, and in addition hand over any information he has on the robbery of the Piemonte-Sardegna bank and on the relations that have been forged between the ultra-leftist groups and the gangsterism now rife in Italy.

11 June

The boss of the publishing house has read *La Repubblica*, which the publicist passed on to him, and is worried. He asks the in-house lawyer and the publicist to come and confer with him in his office.

'Are we not allowing ourselves to get drawn into a very nasty business?' he demands to know.

The lawyer seeks to temper the discussion.

'It is true that in Italy Romano Sebastiani is an influential public prosecutor, with close ties to the Italian Communist Party, or what's left of it, and we certainly shouldn't take his words lightly. At the same time, like all communist sympathisers, he's innately hostile to the Red Brigades, one of whose former leaders apparently appears and is treated sympathetically in the novel, *Escape*. This perhaps explains his annoyance. But what is clear from this opinion piece is that the Italian courts have no evidence against our author. Filippo Zuliani's jailbreak is the one established fact, but it's not a big deal when set against the bank robbery and the assassinations. And when it comes to the shootings, Sebastiani clearly has nothing to go on. A novel is not proof that can be used as evidence in court. As long as it is nothing but a moralising diatribe, no one's in any real danger.'

The boss remains cautious.

'I'd like to think this is the case, but as I see it, someone in Italy is firing a warning shot. Public prosecutors don't, on the whole, amuse themselves by writing gratuitous opinion pieces, and they don't tend to open hostilities unless armed. I fear what is in store.'

Adèle is much more upbeat: 'The book's doing well, very well. Sales are still growing and I've been assured that it will be shortlisted for the Goncourt and Renaudot prizes this autumn. The literary establishment's recognition of a book

that is controversial is a real *tour de force*. It gives us the opportunity to launch an autumn sales drive and get it back into all
the bookshops. This was undreamt-of – it's a title we published
too close to summer, a bit haphazardly, and we've already sold
70,000 copies. If we win a prize, we'll top 200,000. Now is not
the time to stop pushing. If our lawyer gives us the green light,
I can circulate Sebastiani's piece, very discreetly, of course,
invoking the defence of freedom of artistic expression, that
sort of thing…'

'How is your author responding? Can you rely on him? Can
he cope with the pressure? No danger of him slipping up?'

'Filippo? I don't think he keeps up with it all.'

'Doesn't he read the Italian papers? All the refugees do.'

'No.' Adèle shakes her head in a ripple of bleached blond
hair. 'Not him. He's perfectly happy in his bubble and that's
where he wants to stay. I get the impression that he's not interested in Italy, and he tells me he's starting a new book. He
hasn't said what it's about but it will be very different from his
first novel. I'm not convinced he's got a second novel in him,
but we'll see…'

'So let Sebastiani stew. I repeat: there's no need to panic.'

The publisher allows himself to be persuaded.

'All right, we'll carry on.'

But he is still worried. He thinks for a moment then places
a hand on Adèle's arm.

'Don't leave your protégé in complete ignorance of his
success. I think the best policy is to give him a bit of an ego
boost. You know what writers are like … And you're so good
at doing what's needed.'

He rises and the meeting is over. By way of a conclusion, he
says, 'I'm going to take a few precautions, just in case – hang
around the corridors of power a bit and say hello to some old
friends before everyone goes off on holiday, test the water, put
out feelers. After all, we have a president who's a man of letters.
May as well make the most of it.'

Second fortnight in June

Somehow, the news of *Escape's* growing success and of its chances in the scramble for a book prize reach the ears of the Italian cognoscenti, where it causes a stir. It is picked up by all the media, and the press goes on the warpath. Journalists throw caution to the winds. Their main gripe is inspired by Romano Sebastiani's point, which they reiterate: the French are showing appalling judgement in mistaking something that is no more than a shameless commercial exploitation of a heinous event for a sign of literary talent, without any consideration for the suffering of the victims' families. The freedom of expression argument is a pathetic smokescreen that does not conceal the moral bankruptcy of a criminal (because the author is a criminal beyond all doubt, even though his crime is not specified) attempting to flee justice at home. Police mug shots of Filippo Zuliani, full face and in profile, have conveniently found their way into the editorial office, and appear alongside those of the widows of the *carabiniere* and the security guard with their children, shown leaving the church after Sunday mass. The effect is compelling. This is the perfect opportunity for the Italians, so often annoyed and wounded by the intellectual arrogance of the French, to claim the moral high ground, and they have no compunction in exploiting it. The publishing house starts to receive hate mail, mainly written in Italian.

On 22 June, a thunderbolt. A new witness has spontaneously presented himself at a Milan police station. He states that he saw Filippo Zuliani in the company of two men at 14.15 in La Tazza d'Oro, a bar two hundred metres from the Piemonte-Sardegna bank in Via Del Battifolle, on the day of the hold-up by Carlo and his gang. After checking up on the story, the police consider this testimony to be valid. So the status of Filippo Zuliani, seemingly present at the scene of the heist after all, changes from that of indiscreet writer to potential accomplice.

24 June

In Paris, preparations for action are afoot in the publishing house. The boss holds a crisis meeting in his office with, as ever, the lawyer and the publicist. The lawyer considers this testimony to be far-fetched but the publisher, clearly worried, feels that it would be advisable to contact and discuss the matter with their Italian connections before taking any decisions. And they need to act fast, because it will soon be impossible to get hold of anyone.

The lawyer telephones his Milanese colleague and tasks him with a fact-finding mission. The Italian lawyer calls his contacts in various police departments and phones back later that day.

'It's a fact. Following this new statement the police are now seeking to establish Filippo Zuliani's presence outside the Piemonte-Sardegna bank at the time of the robbery.'

'How can this witness have such a precise memory of the day and the time more than a year after the event?'

'He was in the bar waiting for his appointment with a major client at 14.30. Appointment confirmed by the client in question. At 14.15, he asked for his bill, went to the toilet, and came across a very agitated guy vomiting into a washbasin. He watched him while he himself urinated and washed his hands. The man washed his face, then did a few breathing exercises to calm himself down. They left the toilets together, and, while he paid his bill, the other man went to a table at the back of the bar where two men whom our witness couldn't see clearly were waiting for him. Our witness left, had his meeting, and left his client's office at around 16.30. By that time the area was in a state of siege, and the hold-up had taken place. The date is therefore certain.'

'Fine, but why now?'

'Because he never suspected that there was a connection between the hold-up and the incident in the café until a few days ago, when he saw the photos of Filippo Zuliani in all the papers. Then he recognised the agitated customer from the Tazza d'Oro, and decided it was his duty as an upstanding citizen to tell the police what he had seen.'

'What's the name of this providential witness?'

'Daniele Luciani.'

'Who is this guy? Do we know anything about him? I mean is he a regular police informant… ?'

'I understand what you're saying. Our firm has no information on Daniele Luciani. Do you want us to see what we can find?'

'Yes, you never know, but without incurring too many expenses. Was it difficult for you to obtain that information?'

'To tell you the truth, not at all. The police were very cooperative, and I think that everything I have just told you will be all over the Italian papers in the next few days.'

'What do you think?' asks the publisher who has been standing next to the lawyer, listening in on the telephone conversation.

'Pretty worrying, I'm not going to pretend otherwise. I don't believe a word of this statement, and that is precisely what is so worrying. The police can fabricate ten similar accounts whenever they want. And if that's what they're up to, they must have a motive that we are unaware of, and they can continue to do so when it suits them.'

'I just don't understand. Why attack a novel, and why now?'

'A novel, yes, but not just any novel, as you well know. Surely it's about the threat of it winning a major prize? It could well be that it is construed as an unacceptable provocation.'

'Possibly, but not very convincingly so. The Italians have never taken an interest in French literary prizes before.'

A pause. The boss drums his fingers on his desk.

'We may well have made a mistake in pushing this book, I admit. Right…' he turns to Adèle, '…for our part, from today, hold back on *Escape,* and let's protect ourselves as far as possible from any controversy. I think it would be wise to take immediate precautions and have the book removed from the prize entries.'

'You're giving in without a struggle in the face of what is effectively blackmail, censorship even. That's a dangerous attitude,' responds the publicist.

'Give me a break, we're among friends here, spare me that kind of talk. The book has already had a good innings, we've made a lot of money, and I trust you to ensure it continues to do well, even without a prize. So, if we can minimise the risks to ourselves ... and, by the way, there's no point talking to Zuliani about this prize business, he doesn't know what's going on.'

A pause, and he turns back to the lawyer. 'I have the feeling there's something else going on with the Italians, and I don't know what. I find it worrying.'

'Tell me straight – did your author kill the *carabiniere* and the security guard, as he describes in his novel?'

'To be absolutely honest, since you ask me, I have no idea. And as I am neither chief superintendent nor judge, I don't want to know. My problem is different. I have interests in Italy, relationships with authors, publishers, journalists, a whole lot of people. I publish several Italians, I love the place. I don't want to risk ruining all that. I'm very upset by the hate mail we're getting at the moment, several letters a day, every day. So if there is a war between France and Italy over Filippo Zuliani, it's not our publishing house that's going to wage it.'

'Fine. At least, in that respect, your position is clear. But let's not rush into things. I'm not certain we are already on a war footing. It could just be the police and the media getting carried away during the summer news vacuum. Let's wait until we have more information from our Italian colleagues. On the other hand, I do think it's important to inform your author now of the latest developments in Italy. He'll find out one way or another and you need to be assured that he won't panic and vanish into thin air, which would be an understandable reaction on his part but regrettable for us.'

'True.' The boss turns to Adèle, who is a bit out of her depth and has kept quiet since the publisher put her in her place so brusquely.

'You'll take care of that, won't you?'

'Of course,' she replies, resigned.

'Our lawyer says there's no rush. I'd like to think not, but don't leave it too long, it's already the end of June.'

'It's top of my to-do list.'

25 June

Filippo hangs around as June draws to a stormy close. The great machine of Paris literary life is beginning to slow down. Journalists are thin on the ground, writers too, and all important decisions are put off until the end of August, early September. He has far fewer gigs, and misses the thrill of constantly performing, now that he is used to the role. The heat soon becomes suffocating in his little studio flat in Neuilly, despite the proximity of the Seine and the Bois de Boulogne. He feels alone, demobbed and forsaken. Time drags out interminably. He is bored. In this great emptiness, he keeps brooding over the scene in the Café Pouchkine, the dark wood table and the two glasses of vodka, in the twilight, his ears buzzing, he can barely hear Cristina's voice, cannot register what she says, his heart racing. He relives the panic that seized him, overwhelmed him, when she placed her hand on his, propelling him out of the Café Pouchkine, far away from her. A salutary panic, survival reflex. But he lost Cristina.

This morning, on arriving home from work, he finds a note slipped under his door. Glances at the signature: Cristina Pirozzi. Hot flush, surge of hope. He reads, 'I'm away until 26 July. Pay the rent for July and June together. If you need access to the apartment (mains switch, leak, etc.), I've left the keys with the security guard.' No hello or goodbye, usual signature. A frosty note, an overwhelming disappointment. *What did I expect? She also remembers our last meeting at the Café*

Pouchkine. She invited me, we were supposed to drink to my success – she did a whole seduction number, took my hand and I ran away. She doesn't get it. She can't get it. And I didn't try and explain. I've lost her. For good. He slides the note between two books on the shelf and goes to bed.

The stuffy studio apartment is too hot. Sleep punctuated by jumbled and oppressive dreams in which the image of Cristina is mixed up with scenes from the prison. Guards and fellow prisoners are brushing against him, jostling him. Strangely, they are all somehow Cristina. They beat him. He runs and escapes. Then during the exercise period Cristina confronts him alone in the prison yard, and attacks him with a screwdriver. He feels nothing, but it is Carlo who falls into his arms, dead, the screwdriver through his heart. His hands are sticky with blood. Cristina shouts at him, 'You killed Carlo.' He is no longer certain that the body is that of Carlo, or that he is in the prison yard. Cristina leans over the corpse which could be Carlo's, her chignon comes undone and her long, coppery hair brushes his bloody hands. Is she Cristina or the girl who kissed Carlo in the mountains? At this point, he prefers to wake up. The presence of the live Cristina alongside the dead Carlo in the same dream, the confusion between Cristina and the girl in the mountains is deeply disturbing. He waits, his eyes wide open, for the images to recede, to fade, and lose their oppressive intensity. He convinces himself that he will forget them, that he has already forgotten them, then gets up, takes a cold shower and makes himself a very strong coffee.

27 June

Adèle invites Filippo to lunch at a restaurant in Saint-Germain that is a favourite haunt of the Paris publishing world. She says she has something she needs to discuss. Filippo is delighted to accept her invitation. He sees her less frequently now, and he realises he misses her. She has become part of his lifestyle.

He arrives at the restaurant where he is clearly expected. A maître d'hôtel holds the big swing door open for him and, without a word, shows him to his table. The restaurant's interior has been carefully designed to meet the needs of its clientele. In the vast dining room, all the tables are hedged by antique mahogany partitions at half-height and topped with copper rails, so conversations can take place in complete privacy. But the partitions are just low enough for diners to see who comes in, with whom, and who goes to sit where.

The table Adèle has reserved is at the very back of the restaurant, and so the maître d'hôtel has him cross the entire room. Conversations stop as he passes. And the same whispers can be heard from one table to the next.

'Did you see who just came in? Filippo Zuliani.'

'I can understand why Jeanne Champaud fell head-over-heels for him. He's such a cute and charming young man.'

'Have you read *Escape*? Apparently it's in the running for a prize.'

'Overrated.'

'First novel, let's wait for the second.'

'The gamble's certainly paid off for the publisher.'

They have reached the table. The maître d'hôtel pulls out the chair, Filippo sits down and orders a Perrier with a slice of lemon. Talk at the other tables has resumed.

Adèle, pirouetting from table to table, greeting people, stopping for a word here, a smile there, waves at him across the room: 'I'm here, I'm coming'. He nods and quietly digests what has just happened: nothing less than his entrance into the literary world. Recognition from readers, recognition from people in the industry, can he still have any doubts?

Adèle puts off coming over to their table and starting a conversation that she knows will be tricky. The lawyer warned that Filippo might panic and run away or even disappear. What should she do in that case? She finally brings herself to sit down facing him, with a smile.

'I'm working on your behalf.' She contemplates the glass of Perrier. 'You're drinking water?'

'I've only just woken up.' Slight embarrassment.

'Oh … true. Of course.' She doesn't look at the menu, she knows it by heart.

'I recommend the veal chop with spinach. It's one of their signature dishes.' She signals to the waiter. 'Two veal chops, Henri. And a Saumur-Champigny, as usual.'

Slowly she unfolds her white napkin. Now to prepare him for the bad news. First of all, flatter the ego of the man and the writer. An age-old female ploy which, curiously, still works. She leans towards Filippo.

'Let's talk business. Did you hear the whispering when you came into the restaurant?'

He laughs.

'Yes. I felt as though I was being wafted to the table by the buzz.'

Adèle glances at him covertly from beneath her fringe. *Cleverer than he'd have me believe.*

'Your book is number two in this week's bestseller list.' A pause, no reaction from Filippo. 'And it's still on the up. I had a call from Pivot's secretary. It looks as though you'll be a guest on his September programme.'

Filippo still says nothing, he has never heard of Bernard Pivot, and has no idea of the audience that a book programme like *Apostrophes* attracts. Adèle takes Filippo's silence for an affectation of cool, which makes her task harder, and goes on, dropping her voice.

'Are you aware that you're now a bestselling author?'

'Yes, I've just realised that. Only one question: are you sure that there hasn't been a mistake, that it really is me?'

She stares at him, bemused. Too bad, she has to carry on – it's what she came here to do.

'I've also got to talk to you about Italy. It's not such good news on that front. To be brutal, the Italian press is accusing you of being an accomplice – the word makes Filippo bristle – in the fatal Piemonte-Sardegna bank hold-up in Milan and of being a fugitive from the Italian justice system. You look surprised. Don't you read the Italian press?'

'No, I don't.' He has regained his composure and is smiling blissfully. 'They're saying that I'm an accomplice. Are those the words they use?'

She realises that in all the time she's known him, she's never seen him smile like that, with a sort of calm assurance. What had the lawyer said? Wasn't he supposed to panic?

'Yes, that's what they're saying. Aren't you worried?'

'Why should I be? I tell a story set in Italy, the Italians are interested in it, and what's more, they fall for it. They find the story convincing, they even think and say it's true. I think that's brilliant, don't you?'

'Maybe … well, I don't know…'

'As a writer I felt a fraud, I needed some sort of endorsement, and I'm getting it from Italy, I couldn't dream of more.'

Adèle is flummoxed by his reply. She clings to her role as hostess and refills their wine glasses. An oblivious guy, unpredictable. She is completely out of her depth in this situation, but she has delivered the message, so mission accomplished. Not long till the holidays. She relaxes, and hastens the end of the meal.

The minute she has finished her coffee, Adèle makes her getaway. 'Other urgent meetings … We'll touch base soon. Are you staying in Paris over the summer? I'll call you.'

Filippo makes his way back to Neuilly on foot along the banks of the Seine and the Champs-Élysées, a glorious walk, which takes him nearly two hours. He is a writer, someone people talk about, who has flesh-and-blood readers – he's met them. He feels light, walks rhythmically and smiles at passersby in summer dress who cross his path. He has told a simple story in his own words, a story in which he is neither betrayed nor abandoned, a story with friends and accomplices, one whose pace he controls. He gives a passing girl the eye, without slowing down. *An accomplice of criminals*, the words go round and round in his head. *Accomplice*, an echo of the press articles he'd read in Bologna, over a year ago. 'Accessory to a jailbreak … Accessory to a bank robbery…' At the time the word and the thing had felt too heavy to bear, and he fled Bologna in a panic, as he later fled the Café Pouchkine. But now, no more frantic running away. He has found his place, that of the accomplice, and he is recognised for what he says he is. He's come to terms with it.

He is relieved, relaxed. Elated, he walks faster past the Champs-Élysées gardens, walks with a dance in his step, humming to himself, on this wonderful June day, in this beautiful city. He, Filippo Zuliani, has an extraordinary power. What he has written is real. Not the truth, much more than that: reality. Or its opposite. He becomes a little muddled, but it doesn't matter, he is happy.

On entering his building, he looks at himself in the mirrors in the lift, and smiles at his reflection. Attractive guy, the accomplice. Once inside his flat, Filippo showers, puts on a T-shirt and pours himself a large glass of cold water. His gaze lights on Cristina's note, sitting on the bookshelf. Away until 26 July. So the apartment next door is empty. The apartment Cristina has never invited him to enter. He remembers their first meeting, in the hall, the polite handshake, her distant smile, and his disappointment then bitterness – the fleeting temptation to steal things from her, objects she'd left just within his reach, and to run away. Out of revenge. That was over a year ago. He's moved on since, perhaps, but … Once he had dreamt of sitting beside her, in her apartment, at her desk. Then came the Café Pouchkine episode, the missed opportunity, his loss of control, running away. And today, '*If you require access to the apartment…*' An invitation. A sudden urge to break in, to invade Cristina's territory and leave his mark there. Accomplice. He not only has the urge, he has the ability.

He rummages in the kitchen drawer for an instrument with which to force the lock, and finds a slim screwdriver. He picks it up, looks at it and toys with it. There's no mistaking it, this is the screwdriver from his dream, the one Cristina used to attack him in the prison yard – the one that stabbed Carlo through the heart. Break open Cristina's door with the weapon that killed Carlo. A flash of anxiety, a flash from his dream. Then he shakes himself and goes to the door of Cristina's apartment. He hasn't lost the knack, the door gives way within moments. He stands on the threshold of the vast living room, holding his breath. No alarm, a glance round the room, no sign of CCTV cameras, the feeling that his intrusion is accepted. Desired?

As a reflex he closes the front door, jams the lock with the screwdriver for peace of mind, then takes two steps forward and looks slowly about him. Dark wooden flooring, silky smooth, designed to be walked on barefoot, white walls, two big bay windows that probably look out on to a veranda, closed off by blinds that allow minimal light to filter through the metallic slats. The dining room on the left, steel and glass furniture, sitting room on the right, bookshelves taking up an entire wall, black-and-white leather armchairs, and on a coffee table beside a ponyskin and steel chaise longue that is the ultimate in lightness and elegance, is a familiar-looking blob of colour. He goes over to it. Guidoriccio da Fogliano, the lone conqueror, features on the cover of a heavy tome. He had forgotten him ever since he began his new life, and here he is, grabbing him again. Filippo is completely shaken. There's no such thing as coincidence, but the gods move in mysterious ways. Black letters spell out the book's title: *Siena*. He leans over and opens it. On the flyleaf, a brief handwritten dedication: 'To Cristina, so that during your exile in Paris you won't forget the magical city where we met.' A signature he doesn't attempt to decipher. He tells himself that perhaps he's jealous, and the thought amuses him. He flicks through a few pages, lots of photos of a red-and-brown brick city, which leave him with a taste of death in his mouth. A dozen photos of Guidoriccio and the surrounding landscape speak of conquests, in a language he knows well. He puts the book back on the coffee table, leaving it open at the double-page spread devoted to 'Guidoriccio da Fogliano', in all his majesty.

On a trolley within his reach are bottles of spirits and glasses. He selects a brandy, because he has never had one before, fills a balloon glass to the brim and takes a large gulp. He hesitates. *Too rough? Too sweet? Too strong.* He leaves the glass three-quarters full beside the book, goes out of the sitting room, through a door and finds the bedroom and then the dressing room, lined with dark wood. A shelf houses a collection of hats on wooden stands. He takes one down and holds it, a weird bunch of pink and white flowers with a white tulle veil. He holds it at eye level and Cristina is there in front of him, her chignon half undone. He helps her adjust her hairpins, scoop up the coppery mass, place the flowers on her hair and lower the veil over her face, blotting it out. A smile behind the veil, charm he would sell his soul for, then she disappears.

He drops the floral hat on to the floor and goes into the bathroom and switches on the light. Vast. To the left, a huge mirror lit by eight bulbs, like the ones he has sometimes seen in hair salons, a dressing table cluttered with pots, tubes and jars, and an armchair. He sits down, picks up a bottle and opens it. A fragrance. He remembers. In Rome, the stakeouts in front of the perfumeries of the Via Veneto where they used to select wealthy customers in the shops, await them at the exit, follow them in the street and snatch their bag at the first opportunity. He recalls the pleasure he felt watching them, on the other side of the window, in that luxurious, feminine world, their slow, restrained, balletic movements in tune with those of the sales assistants, the way they inclined their heads and closed their eyes to inhale the fragrance of a drop of perfume on the back of their hand, their smiles. They lived and moved in another world, and he dreamt that one day he would take the arm of one of those elegant women, instead of snatching her bag, that together they would walk up the Via Veneto, hips touching, steps chiming, that they would walk past an admiring gang of hooligans standing against the wall, *Did you see how he picked up that rich bitch?* and that she would introduce him to the luxury world of expensive women, the ones who smelt good.

He spins out the dream. He toys with a bottle, knocks it over, rights it, removes the stopper and rubs it on the back of his left hand, as he'd seen the women doing inside the shop, and the subtle fragrance greets him. He says aloud, 'Mitsouko, by Guerlain', and closes his eyes. And now ... He replaces the stopper and puts the scent bottle in his pocket, gets up, switches off the light, returns to his flat, lies down on the bed and slips the bottle of perfume under the pillow. The dream machine starts up, expensive women, war and conquest, the story is already there at his fingertips. Exhilaration. Above all, don't lose the thread. Start writing again. He has no more doubts, no more anxiety. With words, everything is possible. Writing, the weapon of victory. He is no longer bored.

CHAPTER SEVEN

END OF JUNE–JULY 1988, FRANCE–ITALY

27 June

Lisa stays up late every night, working at home, at her desk. She files the documents she has gathered on what is now the Filippo Zuliani affair, formerly the Carlo Fedeli affair. She discards articles that dwell on the two adorable Barbieri kids, children of the *carabiniere* shot during the hold-up on 3 March 1987, not to mention the little Gasparini girl, the security guard's daughter killed in the same tragic circumstances – a sweet six-year-old child with golden curls. She retains everything on Daniele Luciani, the providential witness who belatedly came forward and accused Filippo. She keeps any articles or information she can glean from here and there, and through consulting numerous directories. In short, not much. This Daniele Luciani leaves no traces beyond an address in Milan that seems to be just a PO box and a telephone number that no one answers, no identifiable occupation, no photos, no direct contact with the press. She feels she has reached the same impasse as last year when she was trying to find out about Brigadier Renzi. It is an impenetrable ball of interwoven lies, from which she is unable to disentangle a single thread. For Lisa, there is absolutely no doubt – this morass is the hallmark of the Italian secret service, the most efficient institution in the entire country. It is now twenty years since it set itself the goal of smashing the communists' influence. Something that back then was a matter of urgency, for the Communist Party was on the brink of being democratically elected to power, an intolerable prospect both for the Italian establishment and for America. And now they are achieving that goal through bomb attacks, massacres, and a whole array of dirty tricks. *Faced with that, we on the far left, including prisoners, exiles, those turned informers, others who have dissociated themselves, or the desperate and the confused who carry on killing without knowing why: we're incapable of coming to terms with our defeat and of salvaging our past.*

She stands up, exhausted, tempted to give up. Leaning on the sill of the open window, she drinks a good, strong coffee in tiny sips to allow the flavour to explode in her mouth. *I mustn't let them crush me. What I need is method. First of all, one thing's clear, I'm not the only person responsible for that entire history. And that's something I need to tell myself over and over again, as often as necessary. Right now, my sole aim is to shed light on Carlo's death. For myself first of all. With the publication of that novel, it's become a personal matter. The weight of the past is already so heavy with recurrent nightmares, exile, suffering and defeat, I need at least to hang on to the conviction that the struggle was worth waging and that I went through it at the side of the man I loved. If my soulmate of nearly twenty years of impassioned and devastating political battles is to be deemed no better than a bandit, I'll have nothing left of my past life or my personal history. But I'm not just fighting for myself and for Carlo. Nor was I fighting for abstract ideas. Life, each person's memory, is a valuable treasure. Our collective destiny is woven from all our individual lives, and each one of us must be defended by all. Stay strong.*

She returns to her desk. Go back to square one. Initially, the chain of events is clear. January '87, open letter from the Red Brigades saying, 'We are defeated, we are laying down our arms, we need to take stock of the past collectively and accept ourselves for who we are, the protagonists of this history.' Unacceptable in an Italy fragmenting amid the scandal of the P2 Masonic Lodge, the wholesale corruption of politicians, the mafia, the decline of the Communist Party. The entire edifice was so shaky that the Red Brigades, together with the entire far left of the '60s and '70s, had to remain the unifying scapegoat, or better, the external enemy. So something had to be done: the invention of the concept of 'dissociation' with the introduction of a special law, Carlo's escape, and the entire sting operation that would result in Carlo being labelled a criminal and executed. During this sequence of events, the Red Brigades' splinter group, the Union of Combative Communists – manipulated or not, it amounts to the same thing – kill Lando Conti, the former mayor of Florence shortly after the aborted robbery and Carlo's death, both possible triggers. Any political debate about the Red Brigades' declaration is well and truly nipped in the bud. Mission accomplished, according to police procedure.

Then this crackpot Filippo turns up. He tells a story that plays right into the hands of the Italian secret service, because it not only turns Carlo into a bank robber but into the leader of a Milanese gang caught up in a turf war with a Roman gang to boot. A story that legitimises the police version of events. So why are they hounding him? Suddenly, a new question occurs: are they hounding him or are they stirring things up, raising his profile? Is Filippo a secret service mole? Obviously the question has to be asked. Why is she asking it now? At a complete loss, Lisa gets up, goes back over to the window and stares at the dark silhouettes of the trees against the purple Parisian night sky. Claustrophobia, paranoia, need a breather. Phone Roberto? Not at this hour, it's too late.

Three discreet taps at the door. She goes over to open it.

'Pier-Luigi…'

She is surprised. A young Italian refugee whom she has frequently seen at Sunday meetings, but they have never spoken.

'What are you doing here? Who gave you my address?'

'Roberto. May I come in?'

She hesitates for a moment. Then, 'Why not? Good timing,

I've just made some coffee. But not too long, it's late and I'm tired.' He settles himself into the big armchair by the coffee table and she brings over two cups of coffee and a few biscuits. Then he blurts out: 'I knew nothing about Brigadier Renzi last year. I would have liked to help you, but I couldn't. Now, it's different. I know who Daniele Luciani is. Does that interest you?'

'Obviously.'

Pier-Luigi speaks as if leading a commando operation. Precise and concise.

'An extreme right-wing activist. A member of the terrorist wing of Ordine Nuovo. He was implicated in the Brescia massacre.'

Shocked, Lisa sits down in the armchair facing him and closes her eyes. *Calm down, breathe. Don't forget, you don't know this guy. Anything's possible.*

'OK, let's take this slowly. How do you know this?'

'I used to know Luciani well. I'm from Brescia, from a banking family with fascist leanings. Before the war my father was a staunch supporter of Mussolini whom he considered as the only possible bulwark against the reds and the mafia. He didn't change his mind after the war either. My elder brother, Andrea, was one of the founders of the terrorist organisation Ordine Nuovo. The Brescia group used to meet in the shed at the bottom of our garden. My brother was in charge of liaising with the Padua Ordine Nuovo group. Delfo Zorzi, who was later accused of being involved in the Brescia bombing, often used to come to the house. And so did others.'

'Including Daniele Luciani?'

'Yes, including Daniele Luciani, who was called Bonamico in those days.'

Lisa feels dizzy, in need of something to hold on to.

'Let's start again, from the beginning.'

'For me, the beginning was the Brescia anti-fascist demonstration of 28 May 1974.'

Lisa nods, she knows about it.

'I had just turned eighteen.' He stops abruptly, a happy memory, a guilty little smile: 'Like in the song.' He sees that Lisa is baffled and goes on: 'I was finding it harder and harder to bear the atmosphere at home, my father's harsh authoritarianism, my mother's frivolity and submissiveness. I loved, or I thought I loved, a woman much older than me and I couldn't tell anyone about her. I dreamt of a different world, and I believed we Italians were in the process of building it. I went to the anti-fascist demo in Brescia. My first demo.' Another pause. 'It's funny how life can change dramatically, without you really having decided...'

'Keep going.'

'I was on the other side of the square when the bomb went off under the arcades. I was looking elsewhere, I didn't see anything, but I heard the explosion. Massive. Afterwards, for one or two seconds, an eternity of total silence, I thought I'd gone deaf, and then all I could hear were screams of panic, and I was swept along by the crowd surging down the side streets, trying to get away from the site of the explosion. After a while, I managed to calm down and make my way back to the square. I wanted to see and take in what had just happened. There were ambulances everywhere. The dead and the gravely wounded were being evacuated. On one side of the square an emergency medical team was tending to the less seriously injured. The fire brigade was hosing down the site of the explosion with powerful jets, removing all the rubble and with it all traces of the bomb, helped by a group of young men – my brother and his friends. Including Daniele Bonamico. I watched them from a distance. Afterwards, they left, laughing and clapping each other on the back. Happy. When the forensic team arrived, an hour later, there was nothing left to analyse. No one ever found out who gave the fire brigade the order to clean up the debris. Suspects among neo-fascist groups were arrested, including my brother, but they weren't held for long. All the trials ended up being dismissed for lack of evidence. The final one was last year.'

Lisa, irritated, *stop wasting time.*

'I know all that.'

'I became obsessed with the sight of the dead and wounded. I was convinced that my brother and his friends had planted the bomb. That summer I left my family and Brescia for good, without saying anything – the act of a coward. I went to Milan to study. As soon as I got there, I joined Lotta Continua, which dissolved itself shortly afterwards. I felt as though I was losing my family a second time. I was very young, with no political training, and I did a lot of stupid things. I looted shops, attacked police stations, perhaps worse, and then I ended up here...'

'What about Daniele Bonamico?'

'I never saw him again. And I've never resumed any contact with any member of my family. I was very fond of my two sisters, and really missed them. That's the way things are where I come from. If you stray, you're dead to your family. I found out later from a classmate I met up with in Milan that Daniele had kept in touch with Andrea for a while, and then he and my brother had a falling out, apparently a violent one. I don't know why. Daniele reportedly had to leave Brescia. Then he changed his name. When my friend ran into him in Milan, he was called Luciani, and he pretended not to recognise him. I discovered all that some time ago, by chance, and I didn't think anything of it until I saw Daniele Luciani's name in the papers.'

'So, in your view, he could be playing the agent provocateur?'

'I didn't say that, and I have no idea. I've told you what I know for certain. And what I've heard trusted friends say. No more.'

'Let's suppose that this Daniele is working with the cops. If Filippo has a genuine alibi for the time of the bank robbery, people will say that the cops mistook a novel for real life and they'll look ridiculous.'

'But they know he hasn't got an alibi.'

'What do you mean?'

'You said so yourself at the Sunday meeting just after the book came out, over a month ago, don't you remember? What do you imagine? That everything said in those meetings remains confidential?'

Lisa sinks deeper into her chair, hands pressed together, her face burning, and says very quietly: 'It's true. You're right.'

After a long silence: 'Do you have any proof of what you're saying?'

'No. I've told you what I know, and I don't intend to start again. I came to see you because I admire your courage and your obstinacy. You never give up. There's something classy about that. I'm different. I've found a real job I like at last, in Brittany. I'm going to move there, and it's goodbye to Italy and the Italians. I don't want to be accountable to anyone, do you understand? I just want to forget. It's been nothing but calamity. As for the proof, you'll have to sort that out yourself.'

It is long past midnight, Lisa and Roberto are still at their usual table in their favourite Chinese restaurant on the corner of the Rue de Belleville. Even at this late hour, the service is discreet and fast.

'There, Roberto. I've told you everything. What do you think?'

'Pier-Luigi may be genuine, but he might also be working for the Italian secret service. His departure for a job in Brittany, right after telling you this story … in either case, it means that you're spot on and that Carlo didn't die in a simple bank robbery.'

'Now what?'

'Do you want to drop it?'

'No. Especially not now that I finally have something resembling a lead.'

'Well that sounds obvious. You'll have to dig deeper, until you find something that either confirms or demolishes Pier-Luigi's story. You're our expert in this sort of work, and of course, I'm here if you need a hand with anything specific. Do you know Pier-Luigi's surname?'

'Of course. Tomasino. I didn't need to ask him.'

'Have you memorised the list of all the refugees?'

'More or less.'

'I think you should start with his family. It shouldn't be too hard to find information about a prominent Brescia banking family, if they do exist.'

'Supposing I manage to confirm Pier-Luigi's story?'

'If the cops' surprise witness turns out to be a highly dubious character who was in jail with Carlo and then subsequently changed his name, you've won – the entire hold-up business stinks.'

'So what do we do with that information?'

'We talk to our lawyers first. They've asked us to be cautious and to go through them. The League of Human Rights, the journalists we know, and perhaps the publisher too. We go public, making as much noise as possible. Filippo is now famous enough for the story to make the news. But you have to tell him all this now, discuss it with him, tell him what we know, what we're looking for, and try to get him to agree on the way to conduct this whole thing.'

'I really have no wish to see him. I loathe the guy and I don't understand him. He writes a novel, as of course he's entitled to. What's more, it's a bestseller. Why doesn't he state, once and for all, that he made up the whole story based on a newspaper article and that he has nothing to do with Carlo?'

'Because he does have something to do with Carlo, whether you like it or not. They were cellmates, and clearly, from what I've heard and read, there was a strong bond between them that has nothing to do with politics, and they escaped together. We don't know what happened afterwards. He gives one version of events, which isn't the same as yours. The relationship between reality and fiction is always very complex. But one thing is certain: he shared a cell with Carlo for six months. What happened afterwards, what he felt, what he made up, it's impossible to know. Thousands of people are moved by his story – he himself has ended up believing it. And he's stuck. Not to mention that it might be true ... I sometimes think that he feels guilty towards Carlo, perhaps because he helped him escape, and it ended in tragedy.'

Lisa lets this sink in. She recalls very clearly what she said to Filippo, the one time she met him, a lost kid: *You're to blame for that assassination.* Devastating. No question of sharing this memory with Roberto. She smiles at him and reaches across the table to brush his cheek with her hand.

'I've never understood a thing about men. Too unpredict-able and too irrational for me...'

'You're so stubborn. It's all very well changing the subject, but you're going to have to cooperate with Filippo.'

28 June
Things are slow at the occupational health centre as June draws to a close. Cristina, one of the two doctors, has already gone on holiday and appointments are few and far between. Lisa takes advantage of the lull to bring her address book into the office – the precious address book in which she keeps every contact in media and cultural circles that she's gath-ered over the years and scrupulously kept up to date. Names of all those who have severed communications are crossed out, others are annotated with details of their habits, tastes, weaknesses, favours granted or, more rarely, sought. It is her secret weapon, which she has never shown anyone, not even Roberto. Perhaps a feeling of shame at keeping tabs on her contacts. Armed with her little book she sets out with a sense of excitement, to find contacts who might be able to talk to her about Daniele Bonamico/Luciani. At least when she has a

clear and precise task to occupy her, she forgets the heartache of exile, and feels alive, energetic.

Find a journo in Brescia. The best would be to try the local press to start with, without directly mentioning Daniele Luciani's name, or that of Filippo Zuliani. After twenty or so phone calls, she comes across an 'old friend' in the Socialist Party and a reporter for Canale 5, the television channel owned by Berlusconi, now well on his way up the career ladder. Not yet too proud of being there, and very happy to redeem himself in his own eyes and do a little favour for a reprobate, keeping it quiet of course. He gives her the phone number of his niece, a young journalist who has just been hired as an intern at the *Corriere di Brescia* and is working on the news-in-brief section. 'A real go-getter,' he adds, with a hint of disapproval in his voice. *Just what I need*, thinks Lisa.

Stefania Cavalli has a shrill, almost childlike voice. She listens attentively to Lisa, who mentions her uncle's name and asks if the paper has an archive on the Tomasino banking family that she could pass on to her. Stefania has her repeat the name, and then, without a second's hesitation: 'I'll be straight with you. If I find this information, what do I get in return?'

Lisa smiles. The niece is very different from her uncle. So much the better. What if, as a bonus, she gives Stefania the chance to publicise the affair in Italy? That will save her from having to submit to the lawyers' scrutiny and going to the League of Human Rights in France, as well as avoiding any discussion with Filippo. Tempting.

'I'll be equally straight with you. I'm not going to mix you up in this. I'm not sure of the veracity of my information. But if it is confirmed, which depends on what you dig up, I'll have a scoop. A big one. I'm in France, and have no way of leaving. You'll have an exclusive on the story for Italy, on condition we both agree not to disclose that this conversation took place.'

'Give me an idea what this story's about.'

'The fallout from the Brescia massacre of 28 May 1974.'

'There was a lot of talk about it here last year and a fresh trial, which once again ended up with the case being dismissed.'

'I know.'

'Protecting the sources on both sides?'

'Absolutely.'

'OK, I'm up for it. What exactly do you need to know?'

'Some background on the Tomasino family, without going back to the year dot, just to have an idea of the circles they move in. I'm particularly interested in 1974. Who was arrested in the immediate aftermath of the massacre? Does the name of the eldest Tomasino boy, Andrea, figure on the lists? And a certain Daniele Bonamico? What can we find out about this Bonamico? Does he still live in Brescia, and what is known about his family? You might not find all that in the paper's archives...'

'Probably not, don't worry about me. If this Daniele exists, I'll find him. Is that all?'

'Yes.'

'Give me two days. I'll call you tomorrow evening.'

'After eight, at home. I'll give you my number.'

30 June

Stefania calls at 8.15. Punctual, or almost. Lisa is grateful to her for sparing her the ordeal of waiting.

'Oh, you're there?' There's a hint of laughter in her voice.

'Of course I'm here.'

'Nothing in the paper. It has never published anything on the Tomasino family.' She gives Lisa a moment to digest her disappointment. 'But a whole lot in the archives, particularly unpublished articles. One hell of a family. I'm a newcomer to Brescia, so this gets me into the swing of things. Hold on, let me go back to my notes...'

Lisa grits her teeth. The kid's got a sense of theatre. She says nothing.

'...Here we are. A prosperous family-owned bank until the

war. The grandfather, a notorious fascist, goes off and dies a violent death in the Republic of Salò saga, which denotes either profound stupidity or profound despair. The bank came in for strong criticism after the war, because of its fascist past, and the son's only solution was to allow it to be taken over by the Piemonte-Sardegna bank.' Lisa shudders at the name; could there be a connection? 'He's appointed regional director of the new bank, thus securing a very lucrative position for himself. Married into a prominent Venetian family, four children, two boys, two girls. As for the eldest son, Andrea – named after his grandfather, by the way – he becomes very active in neo-fascist circles. To be precise, Ordine Nuovo, in its clandestine period, is repeatedly hinted at in a number of half-concealed allusions. He's alleged to have been involved in the Padua group, which may explain why he was arrested during the investigation into the massacre of the 28th of May, 1974. He was released a month later, for lack of evidence. A certain Daniele Bonamico was arrested and released at the same time as him.' Lisa's heart is racing, *I'm there, I'm almost there.* 'And in that connection I've got a very funny story (*I don't give a damn about your funny story. Get on with it*), even if it is a bit late in the day. In 1976, Andrea and Daniele have a fight in public, in the main square. A very violent, bare-knuckled brawl. The police break it up and cart them both off to the police station.

According to statements made to the police, Andrea accuses Daniele of having slept with his sister Anna-Maria, without going into further detail, but I bet she ended up pregnant. Daniele offers to make amends by marrying the young lady, but Andrea replies that it's impossible for a Tomasino to marry a hired hand and that's what sets off the fight. Afterwards, the family saga continues, but there's nothing further about Anna-Maria – vanished, swallowed up. But maybe that's not of any interest to you.'

Lisa hears Pier-Luigi, *If you stray, you're dead to your family.*

And what if, in Anna-Maria's case, they had taken it literally? Pier-Luigi, a shy, deeply wounded man. *I should have paid more attention to the guy from the start. A missed opportunity to get to know him. The curse of exile. I'm becoming hardened. No time to lose.* Her attention reverts to Stefania.

'No, it's not. Did you find out anything else about Daniele Bonamico?'

'A few bits and pieces. Only one photo, from 1974, where he's in the background, hiding behind Andrea Tomasino who is showing off in the front row. Scary-looking, with eyebrows that join in the middle, a sinister air, a scar on his cheek that pulls his whole face downwards. Anna-Maria couldn't have had much choice, or else she had strange taste. Girls from good families who have been a bit too sheltered sometimes rebel by falling for a bit of rough. I'm pretty certain that he was no longer in Brescia after 1976. I also dug up some information on his family.'

'Keep going.'

'The grandparents on both sides were farming families from the Po valley. His parents met and married in their village before coming to Brescia.'

'Have you got the names of these families?'

'Hold on a sec.' Lisa hears her flipping through the pages. 'Yes. Grandfather Bonamico married a Farione on one side, and on the other, an Ercoli married a Luciani.'

There is a long silence. Lisa feels a mixture of excitement and incredulity. The young woman grows impatient.

'So, have I got my scoop?'

'Maybe. I think so. Daniele Luciani is the name of the surprise witness who popped up a few days ago in the case of the bank robbery of the 3rd of March 1987 at the Piemonte-Sardegna bank in Milan. He's accusing an Italian writer, a certain Filippo Zuliani, a refugee in France.'

'I know about it, I followed the news. He's not exactly accusing him – he states he was present at the scene.'

'According to a credible source, an eyewitness who knew the Brescia protagonists personally, Daniele Luciani is in fact Daniele Bonamico. In other words, Ordine Nuovo's henchman implicated in the Brescia massacre. This suggests he could have left Brescia and changed his name, adopting that of his grandparents, with dates yet to be established, but it's possible that he chose to remain in contact with the secret service.'

'Yes, with a lot more delving, this could make a good story. I'll take it.'

'I can already see the headline: "Mystery witness turns out to be a Brescia man with a past".'

'No, that's not a good headline. Leave me to do my job. I'll call you back.' And Stefania hangs up.

Night of 2 July

Stefania calls Lisa who is sound asleep. She gropes blindly for the phone and picks it up in the dark.

'The *Corriere di Brescia* refuses to publish anything.' A silence. Lisa is sitting up now, wide awake. 'That's not all. My editor hauled me into the office this morning, even though it's Saturday and we were almost the only people there. The offices were deserted. He grilled me on my sudden interest in Daniele Luciani. I kept it very vague, and he ended up dropping your name, and asked me if I'd been in touch with you. Surprising, isn't it?'

Lisa groans.

'More than surprising. I'd say worrying.'

'I said no, no contact with you, and since he kept pressing me, I ended up giving my uncle's name as the source of my information. After all, he acted as go-between, he can take the blame for it. I wasn't sacked, but almost. In any case, the boss made it very clear that there was no question of the *Corriere di Brescia* getting involved in this story. Back to dogs being run over. So your rather far-fetched story is true, and it's put the cat among the pigeons.' Another silence. 'I wanted to let you know and ask you not to call me again.'

'OK. Thank you.'

Lisa lies on her back, staring at the ceiling, fully awake now. What should she make of the reaction at the *Corriere di Brescia*? First of all, obviously, success. Pier-Luigi's story is pretty much confirmed. *I haven't got the evidence yet, but I know it exists and where to look for it.* And a failure too. *With this aborted attempt to get the* Corriere di Brescia *to run the story, I've alerted our enemies, whoever they are, and they now know that we're on to them and we're getting closer. They're going to be able to take precautions. And that's not going to be good for us. Most likely they'll eliminate Luciani. Serious? No, not very serious, the guy has already testified. All the papers are talking about it, impossible to erase, that's all we need. More importantly, no point now trying to publish our story directly in Italy, the media have been muzzled. We'll have to go via the lawyers and the League of Human Rights, here in France. And therefore through Filippo. Shit.*

Lisa gets out of bed and goes into the kitchenette to make a coffee. She paces up and down, half promises herself that she'll do everything she can to put off the moment when she has to meet him. Roberto will say to her: Because you don't want to share Carlo. *Maybe. So what? I'm entitled to feel that way.*

She sits down at her desk. A shadow, a vague memory lurks in her mind, perturbs her, prevents her from considering the job done and closing the file. She goes back over her notes and begins to reread them. Very quickly lights on that little phrase of Stefania's: the takeover of the Tomasino family bank by the Piemonte-Sardegna bank after the war. She recalls how the name Piemonte-Sardegna had struck her when the young journalist mentioned it. Then they had changed the subject. Was its appearance in a different chapter of the history of the bank involved in the hold-up and Carlo's death pure coincidence? Maybe, maybe not. Best to start from the principle that there's no such thing as chance.

3 July

It is Sunday. Lisa is moping around at home, unable to find a new avenue to explore in her investigation. If she were in Milan ... the prospects probably wouldn't be any better.

The Piemonte-Sardegna bank has a Paris address. Rather than staying there doing nothing, why not use the time to go and check out the bank's Paris headquarters. Imagination works better when it can draw on images, actual places, real people. And besides, a walk through Paris is always enjoyable, it's a lovely day and at least she'll have the feeling she's doing something. She finds herself in the Opéra district, standing in front of a magnificent Haussmann building. A discreet copper plate in the entrance porch indicates that the bank's offices are on the second floor. Lisa looks up, the *piano nobile*, a balcony running its length, high ceilings that she imagines covered in frescos. A fine example of nineteenth-century architecture. Of course. The kingdom of Piedmont-Sardinia, Napoleon III, Italian unity, the annexation of Savoy to France – she recalls a whole string of school essays. These offices testify to many strong links that must exist between French and Italian banks. And so ... French historians might have taken an interest in this bank, one way or another.

Lisa hurries back home to Rue de Belleville, grabs her address book and seeks out a contact in the academic world.

It doesn't take her long. She comes across the name of Vicenzo Rivola, very recently arrived in France, close to the Autonomia Operaria movement from which Lisa, as a good ex-Red Brigades member, keeps her distance. But French intellectuals have great respect for this movement, whose manifestos, journals, books and talks are of a reliably high standard. Vicenzo swiftly succeeded in finding some hours' teaching in the sociology department of a major Paris university. Lisa picks up the phone and easily gets through to him. She explains what she is looking for: any available information on the links between the Piemonte-Sardegna banks and Tomasino after 1945.

'It's a bit vague, but I can't be any more specific. I'm groping in the dark and I don't know what I'm looking for.'

'That's the best way of coming across something new. At my university we have an excellent historian of modern-day banks. A former communist, not too sectarian, an encyclopaedic mind. I don't know him personally, but I can put you in touch. On the other hand, I warn you, it might take him a while to respond. Academics aren't journalists – they're in no hurry.'

Early July

For the last few days, each morning just before six, a man has come and planted himself beneath an awning around fifty metres from the rear façade of the Tour Albassur. He's a sporty type in his mid-thirties, wearing a grey hoodie with no loud logos on it, jeans and trainers. He stands chain-smoking in the shelter of a low concrete wall, his hood pulled down over his face. He carefully stubs out each cigarette on the sole of his shoe, takes a matchbox out of his pocket, crams the cigarette butt in the box and puts it back in his pocket before lighting another one. He perks up when the Albassur security guards on night shift come out, between 6.05 and 6.10, two men in their fifties, chatting. They head for the Métro entrance, walking placidly, bags slung over their shoulders. He watches them until they disappear, then waits another couple of minutes, checks that there is no one near the approach to the tower before departing in the opposite direction, shoulders hunched, hood pulled well down over his eyes.

On the fifth morning, when the two security guards come out of the building, the man peels himself away from the wall, hurries over and speaks to them.

'Excuse me, gentlemen…' The guards stop, wary.

'…I'm sorry to bother you, and I don't want to delay you.

I'm a friend of Filippo Zuliani's. I work at La Défense and I was told he works here too. I'm trying to find him…'

'Too late, mate, he handed in his notice at least a week ago.'

'And you don't know…' The two men have begun to move off, quickening their pace.

'No, we don't know anything. Sorry, mate.'

One of them mutters, 'Dodgy-looking guy!' as they vanish into the Métro. Next morning the lookout is no longer there.

Filippo has begun writing again, feverishly. In order to replay the aborted date at the Café Pouchkine, obliterate the disaster, conquer Cristina. Her magnificent copper hair is like that of the girl Carlo kissed in the mountains, and Filippo loves this game of mirrors and echoes. He wants her, he convinces himself that he needs her because she's rich, beautiful and cultured. He still feels like an imposter in the world he has now entered, constantly playing a part, afraid of betraying a lack of taste or of suffering a memory lapse, liable to be thrown out at any moment. With her on his arm, he would be adopted as a member of the family, and so become truly legitimate. Today, because he has grown up since the Café Pouchkine, he has the strength to conquer – he is no longer the same man. Back then, he was still a petty crook, capable of little more than arousing in her a formidable and mortifying protective instinct. Now he is viewed as the accomplice of an almost legendary criminal, Carlo Fedeli. A much more fascinating character. That makes anything possible. Cristina is attainable.

The best way to set about winning her back is to begin writing again. It is the only pretext he can think of for getting in touch. He works from home, at the kitchen table in his studio flat in Neuilly, barely going out. In front of him is a bottle of Mitsouko, which he caresses from time to time, occasionally removing the stopper and inhaling the fragrance until he feels nauseous. He has tacked Cristina's note saying she'll be away on to the wall, the reverse side facing him, but the message is still clear. When he is stuck, demoralised, can't think of the right words, he contemplates it, and pictures himself in the empty apartment on the other side of the wall, ensconced in an armchair in the sitting room, a notepad on his knees and a glass of brandy close at hand, writing. Sometimes, that is enough to set the dream machine in motion again.

Filippo spends hours wandering disconsolately around Paris, haunting the smartest and most expensive neighbourhoods. He strolls around, nostrils quivering, sniffing out sensations and chance encounters. He likes telling himself he is free to invent his life.

Place Vendôme. He walks around the square, lingering before each shop window. This is the home of Paris's most famous jewellers. He's never been particularly interested in jewellery – he prefers perfume. He stops outside Guerlain. On the other side of the glass, a tall woman has her back to him. A customer. He's mesmerised by her mass of coppery hair, pulled back into a precariously perched chignon, artificially casual, held in place by two big wooden hair slides. He stares at her intricate curls, dreams of caressing the wisps of hair on the back of her neck, of removing the slides one at a time, then burying his face in the cascade of flaming hair finally set free. The woman turns towards him. She has sprinkled a drop of perfume on the back of her hand and inhales it deeply. She hesitates, appears to be considering, takes a few steps, her eyes half-closed, then returns to the counter. She is Italian, he's certain from the way she holds herself, walks and smiles. She picks up a bottle and holds it out to the sales assistant behind the counter. Mitsouko – he recognises the shape. In Rome, he had once furtively peddled dozens of cut-price bottles on the streets around Termini station. He loves little details that resemble echoes, or like signposts mapping out his path. Luciana's coppery hair in the mountains and that of the stranger in Place Vendôme; the bottle of Mitsouko on the Rome streets and at Guerlain.

The woman finishes paying and emerges from the shop. An Italian with coppery hair, that perfume. *Don't stop to think, go for it.*

He walks over to meet her, bows to her, grasps her hand and gives it a ceremonious kiss, without being over-insistent. He says to her in Italian: 'Mitsouko, unless I'm mistaken. An excellent choice.'

She laughs, surprised and amused. Her eyes are amber like her hair. She replies in Italian: 'Yes, of course, Mitsouko. How clever! And how do you know that I'm Italian?'

'Your entire body speaks Italian.'

She cocks her head to one side, with a half-smile. She likes the expression. Filippo continues talking slowly, moving on a few steps.

'Actually, to be completely honest, I've been looking for you in Paris for days...' She follows close behind. Encouraging. '...I needed you, your elegance, your warmth. I've written a book, I wrote it for you, to make you look at me, listen to me, walk beside me, as you are doing now...'

By now they have crossed the entire Place Vendôme. It's in the bag. He stops. '...and so that you'd agree to have a drink with me.'

She stops too, and laughs.

'Around here? Out of the question. The Ritz is full of the wrong kind of people. Rue de Rivoli? Swarming with tourists.'

She hesitates for a moment, torn between curiosity and prudence.

'Why don't we go to my place instead? I live around the corner – just above the Tuileries gardens. I've had a busy day. When you tried to pick me up...'

'I'm not trying to pick you up...'

'Oh really! When you tried to pick me up, I was on my way home. I'd love to go home. It'll be peaceful, I'll make you a tea, and you can tell me about your books.'

When they reach the fifth floor she rummages in her bag. He waits while she finds her keys, opens the door and goes inside. He follows. It is a precious moment; he savours the invitation to enter her private world. Before him is a large, sparsely furnished room, airy and spacious; opposite, three French windows that must open on to a south-facing balcony. The sun filters through the closed lou-vered shutters, which she does not open. A magnificent, dark, highly polished wood floor, white walls, a few items of glass-and-steel furniture around a dining table. A sitting area with squat leather armchairs on steel frames, and a coffee table at the base of a vast bookcase that covers an entire wall.

'Sit down and I'll make the tea.'

She vanishes through the left-hand door into the kitchen. So the bedroom must be off to the right. He sits down, tense, on the alert for the slightest sound, the slightest indication of her presence. She moves around in the kitchen, opens a cupboard, closes it. A sound of cups rattling, water running, then a silence. What is she doing? The water boils. She comes back carrying a tray with two cups and a china teapot on it. She has kicked off her shoes and is walking barefoot on the dark wood floor. He watches her, fascinated by her relaxed manner. He desires her, his throat tight, his muscles paralysed. She sits down facing him and pours black tea into the two cups. He takes a sip of the scalding brew, rises and goes to kneel beside her, removes a slide from her chignon and the edifice slowly collapses – the second slide and her hair cascades down her back. She does not resist, her eyes are closed. He bathes his hand in the silky, slightly damp mass, the scent of warm amber. Can a person die of desire? He stands up, and gathers her in his arms. She is light, and he walks towards the bedroom door, which yields at his touch. In the half-darkness, he makes out the shadowy shape of the bed in the centre of the room, covered in a voluminous white duvet. He lowers her into the hollow of this whiteness and with infinite tenderness leans over towards the face, the mouth, the hair that he has always desired.

He has the beginnings of a story.

18 July

Vicenzo had warned her that things might not move very fast and that academics had no sense of urgency. In July the notion of time is even more elastic. And the long weekend of the 14th of July slows communication down still further. After several phone conversations and a few long explanations, it is only on coming home from work on the evening of Monday 18th July that Lisa finds a package in her letter box. It contains a charming handwritten note from Jacques Chamrousse, professor of contemporary economic history at a Paris university.

Dear Ms Biaggi,

As I said to you over the telephone, I am not an expert on the history of Italian banking. While trying to find the answers to your questions, I came across this book, a history of the Piemonte-Sardegna bank, published to celebrate its centenary, so naturally it has all the drawbacks of this type of publication. But I was able to verify that it is a fairly reliable study, based on numerous established facts, and I hope it contains the information you are looking for. If it doesn't, don't hesitate to contact me again and I'll see if I can find any other more 'orthodox' works. It is an Italian publication, there is no French edition, but of course that won't be a problem for you.

Yours sincerely,

Jacques Chamrousse

Lisa climbs the stairs to her apartment, the book under her arm, and settles down comfortably to skim through it. A beautiful edition with photos of starchy bankers, luxurious offices, lavish, formal commemorations. In 1949, a takeover of the Tomasino family bank, the biggest bank in Brescia and the region. Not a word about its fascist past, but that was only to be expected. The most interesting contribution of the Tomasino bank is its property portfolio, the jewel of which is the building housing the Milan branch of the bank, at number 10, Via Del Battifolle, Milan. What a shock ... That address ... The very one where Carlo was assassinated. And opposite the article, a full-page photo of a magnificent art deco building, in which the bank only occupies part of the ground floor. It was there, on that pavement … Shock makes Lisa burst into tears. She places a trembling hand on the photo, closes her eyes and waits, without moving, until she feels calm again. There is no such thing as chance: this is proof.

A phone call to Roberto: 'SOS, I need your company this evening. I can't be on my own. Haven't got the strength. And no questions.'

Her voice is uncertain and Roberto recognises the signs. They meet at the Chinese restaurant, which always stays open very late. Lisa swings between exhilaration and despondence, underpinned by profound anguish. She grazes rather than eats and downs large amounts of iced tea. Roberto remains calm and waits for her to speak. It is the only thing to be done, he is used to it. After a very long silence: 'Roberto, I need you.'

He smiles.

'Our conversations often begin like this. Can you be more precise?'

'When I told you about Pier-Luigi, you said you could help. You said, "help with anything specific". That's exactly what I need. Help with something specific.'

'So you haven't dropped this Pier-Luigi business?'

Lisa smiles.

'Of course not. Did you really think I'd let it go?'

'I don't know. You haven't mentioned it to me for the last two or three weeks.'

'I'm missing a central piece of the puzzle. Until I have it, I don't want to talk to you about it. You'll say I'm crazy and paranoid.'

'I've never said you're crazy or paranoid.'

'No. But you've certainly thought it. And I don't blame you.'

'So what do you need me to do?'

'I want to know if Carlo ran into a certain Daniele Bonamico or a Daniele Luciani when he was in prison.'

Surprised, Roberto raises his eyebrows.

'I don't know when exactly he changed his name. I didn't ask Pier-Luigi the right question, and it's too late now, he didn't leave me a forwarding address.'

'It's impossible to ask the right questions when you don't know the answers. I didn't know that Luciani was supposed to have met Carlo.'

A silence. Lisa offers no further details.

'Right, tell me what you want me to do.'

'I want you to ask our lawyers to obtain that information. They can easily find out from Carlo's solicitor in Italy. And they promised to help me.'

'Why don't you ask them yourself?'

'Because I don't want to have to answer their questions. I can just picture their faces. "And why do you need this information? What are you up to?" I don't want to say anything until I've got all the information I need. It will be easier for you to say nothing because you don't know anything.'

'Do you badly need to protect yourself, Lisa?'

'Yes, you know I do, and I'm relying on you to help me fend off trouble, as usual.'

'OK. I'll do it tomorrow. Let's go back to your place and have a coffee, it's better than here, and then you can make up a bed for me on the couch – it's much too late for me to go home.'

'Thank you.'

25 July (Monday)

Sitting in the big armchair, his back to the window, Roberto sips an iced coffee.

'There you go. It took a little while, but I finally managed to get the information you want. Daniele Bonamico was in jail at the same time as Carlo in 1986, in the high-security prison. He had the benefit of a reduction in his sentence and was released a month after Carlo's transfer to the second prison.'

Roberto stops speaking. Lisa is ashen, her features hard, set, she is no longer listening. *Exactly the answer I was expecting and I was preparing myself for. Even so, it's a hell of a shock. Carlo, ten years of underground struggle. As a rule the group's logistics ran without a hitch, everything except a bolt from the blue. In prison, the love of my life became the friend of a right-wing extremist, a killer, thinking it was OK to associate with him, that he was apolitical and reliable. What ravages prison can wreak. Worse than exile. When he escaped, Carlo was already dead inside. He fell apart in prison, and I knew nothing about it. My love for him, a huge chapter of our lives in shreds. Will I survive? What for?*

Roberto is growing impatient.

'Enough beating about the bush, Lisa. Now you have to tell me everything you know, what it was that made you ask the right question.'

Lisa starts, then picks up the thread.

'Listen carefully, I'm going to tell you the whole story. Daniele Bonamico is a working-class man from Brescia, on the far right (you're aware that there is such a thing, aren't you?), the sort who get used as goons. He's well in with the Tomasino family, doing dirty deeds with the eldest brother Andrea and involved to some extent in the 1974 massacre – we've already talked about that – but he doesn't know his place and, even though he looks like a low-life thug, he gets one of the Tomasino girls pregnant. He's run out of Brescia by the family. Then he hangs out with the secret service, lends a hand here and there, and ends up in jail with Carlo, before getting himself transferred. I don't know whether Bonamico is already receiving orders, or whether he jumps at the opportunity and negotiates afterwards. I'm inclined to think the latter, but it doesn't matter, the fact is that he becomes close to Carlo. You can imagine how he embroiders the tragic story of his love affair, thwarted by the rich bastards, omitting his political activities, of course. You know Carlo as well as I do. A sentimental romantic and an incorrigible womaniser...'

'And prison is unlikely to have helped, seven years of going without...'

'Once he's understood what makes Carlo tick, Daniele's sitting pretty. He tells Carlo he has a plan for getting his own back on the Tomasinos, obtaining some money and eloping with his beloved. A robbery on one of their old banks, he knows the layout of the premises well from having more or less worked there, and he says he's got contacts inside the bank, people who are prepared to help him, so there's absolutely no risk. It'll go like clockwork, and win them a packet of money to boot. It is even possible that he passed off the girl who was with them as the Tomasino girl. She was in Zuliani's first version of the breakout, the only one I accept as true. All he needs is an accomplice. Carlo's up for it. Just think: an operation to recover loot from the rich to avenge an impoverished lover, involving no violence and no risks, offering him the chance of a new life ... Oh, and the former Tomasino bank is located at number 10, Via Del Battifolle in Milan.'

Roberto winces.

'Are you making this up?'

'No, I'm not making it up. The bank is a former Tomasino establishment, and could be, if I've understood correctly, the Milan head office. To continue. Carlo begins to dream. Then he's transferred, because there's no escape from high-security jails, and Daniele is released a little later. The Red Brigades' open letter gives Carlo the green light. After that, things move very fast. I've always been intrigued by the apparent ease of their escape. From what we know, Carlo had accomplices among the truck drivers, but how did he find them? A mystery. Filippo himself, in his initial account, has no idea. Has anyone investigated? Apparently not. The trucks' pick-up schedule is changed and they're half an hour late. None of the security guards seems concerned, nobody keeps an eye on the rubbish collectors while they load the skip. In my view, I think the only thing that hadn't been planned by the prison management, or by Carlo, is that Filippo gets mixed up in the whole thing. Daniele and the girl are waiting for Carlo at the dump, and drive him to the mountains, carefully concealing themselves from that parasite Filippo. Once they're rid of Filippo, Daniele drives Carlo to the Milan bank. There, once again, it's a cinch, Carlo and his accomplices know the security guards' timetable down to the minute, even though it changes daily. They are anticipated and Carlo is shot down by Brigadier Renzi. Bonamico then takes off and disappears, having fulfilled his contract.'

'I don't believe your story. What about the other two dead, the *carabiniere* and the security guard?'

'I'm not sure about them. They might have been shot to bump up the death toll.'

'I still don't believe it.'

'Why not? Don't you believe our secret service is capable of such murders? How many victims were there in the massacres they organised in league with the far right? Do you think that bothered them in the least?'

'Setting off a bomb and massacring unknown civilians isn't quite the same thing as murdering its own men on an official assignment in cold blood. The political consequences can be much more serious.'

'Really? Wake up, Roberto. Two senior *carabinieri* have just stood trial for the Peteano attack. You remember the Peteano attack? A car bomb blew up a *carabinieri* bus, three *carabinieri* dead. That was in 1972, the *carabinieri* know who planted the bomb as they have concrete evidence. And they cover it up. Until the bomber, an Ordine Nuovo activist, gives himself up, just over three years ago. Well? Isn't that somewhat similar to what I'm saying here?'

'That's the point. Exactly. If they're embroiled in this

business, it's highly unlikely that they'd risk the same tactic just when the trial's taking place.'

'So let's assume that Carlo shot in self-defence when he realised he'd fallen into a trap.'

'Remember, you're always saying that Carlo never used guns, which, by the way, I don't necessarily agree with. More seriously still: how do you explain Bonamico's reappearance as prosecution witness against Filippo? In your scenario, he absolutely has to disappear. He changes his name and he disappears.'

'On that point you're right, it's the fly in the ointment, and I've asked myself the same question. I'd like to know when exactly he changed his name. That would be helpful. To explain his comeback, I wondered whether it might be poor coordination on the part of rival departments. But that's not entirely convincing. And I have a better suggestion. Bonamico was at the scene of the robbery because he was with Carlo, he planned the job with him. Do you follow me? He was seen in the Tazza d'Oro by a witness, who recognised him. You don't forget a mug like that. For example someone who knew him in Brescia at the time of the 1974 bombing, and who knew of his past as a stooge of the neo-fascists. Brescia isn't that far from Milan so it's not out of the question. As I speak, I'm wondering whether this witness too might have a connection with the bank in Via Del Battifolle? A former employee of the Tomasino family, or something. At the time, he's not particularly surprised, but next day after the hold-up, with photos all over the papers, the witness realises that the man he saw with Bonamico in La Tazza d'Oro is the former Red Brigadist. The time of the robbery also fits, and our man does his duty as a citizen and rushes off to tell all to the cops. The cops do nothing, but hush up his testimony. Then comes Filippo's book and the press campaign around him sparked off by Prosecutor Sebastiani, who is definitely not aware of the full picture. Maybe the witness wakes up or something else happens that we don't know about. In any case, by coming forward to testify, Daniele explains his presence in La Tazza d'Oro during the hour prior to the hold-up. He does so without anyone being able to establish a link between him and Carlo, and reinforces the credibility of Filippo's novel, something which suits the police very well.'

'Too complicated.'

'I can't come up with anything better. And if I were Bonamico, complicated or not, I'd be trying to save my skin.'

'When you speak to the League of Human Rights, the lawyers and Filippo, I advise you to stick to the proven facts. The surprise witness is a former fellow inmate of Carlo's under an alias. That's already enough to demolish the official version. As for the rest, I suggest you store it up for the day when you decide to write a novel. In my opinion, you're talented and you've got a subject. When are you seeing Filippo? We need to move fast now.'

'Cristina will be back at work tomorrow. I'll ask her to set up a meeting. She has a better chance of persuading him to come than I do.'

'Promise?'

'I promise.'

CHAPTER EIGHT

27–29 JULY 1988

27 July 1988

Cristina arrives back from New York, where she has spent her holiday with her son, late in the afternoon. She is worn out by the heat, the flight and jet lag, and her spirits are low. She is impatient to get home and settle in. A nice shower, a big glass of fresh water with a slice of lemon, then bed, perhaps with a good novel. Her key turns in the lock, she puts down her suitcase, switches on the light and freezes. The big book on Siena lies open on the coffee table, at the double-page spread on the *condottiere*. Her heart beats faster. For the first time the painting appears as a threat, a declaration of war. Next to it stands the bottle of brandy and a half-filled glass. Evidently someone has been in her apartment. Fear. Maybe still there. Fear. Empty building. Fear. Mounting fear. *Stop. Right now.*

She shakes herself like a wet dog, marches over to the window and opens the blind. She takes a few steps on to the veranda, where the sun still shines in pools, and from the nearby woods there comes a whiff of fresh air: a familiar and reassuring universe. She calms down and goes back inside, inspecting every room meticulously. She picks up the hat from the dressing room floor and replaces it on its stand. She opens all the cupboards. In the bathroom, she tidies the dressing table and notices that the bottle of Mitsouko by Guerlain is missing. Strange. The bedroom seems to have been spared by the visitor.

She returns to the living room, removes the glass from the coffee table, stale: what a waste. Closes the book, relieved to see the menacing warrior disappear. One fresco that she'll never look at in the same way again. Then she picks up the bottle and pours herself a full glass of brandy, more effective on this occasion than water with lemon, and slumps into an armchair. Who has been in her apartment? An immediate certainty: Filippo. Why is she so sure? A thought catches her unawares: *His smell is in this room … Because I know his smell? Have I memorised it? Nonsense. It's simpler than that. I reckon it's Filippo because I know the guy is perfectly capable of forcing my lock – child's play for him. He's a petty crook, and possibly even a killer. Simpler still: because he's an outsider to my world, because I don't understand him, because I toyed with him yet failed to seduce him. I have a burning memory of the way he thrust my hand away when I placed it on his at the Café Pouchkine. A humiliation. Because his running away like that was already an assault. Because he's there, close by, on the other side of the wall, and because that proximity is beginning to feel like a permanent threat of invasion. He's signalling that he can enter my home when he pleases, as he pleases. He is master of my space, and so also of my mental space. I won't live under this threat. First of all, I have to put myself out of his reach. Then, I'll see.*

Cristina stands up, grabs her suitcase still standing by the front door as if waiting for her, and leaves her apartment. She'll spend this first night back in Paris at a hotel.

28 July, Paris

Agences Françaises dispatch

Adriano Sofri, Giorgio Pietrostefani and Ovidio Bompressi, two former leaders and an activist from the Italian ultra-left organisation Lotta Continua, which dissolved in 1976, were arrested in their homes at dawn this morning, and taken to various barracks in Milan. The two leaders are accused of ordering the activist to carry out the assassination of Italian state police official Luigi Calabresi in Milan in 1972.

A summary of the evidence leading to the above arrests: in December 1969, against a backdrop of social unrest, a bomb exploded at the Banca dell'Agricultura, Piazza Fontana, Milan, killing seventeen people and wounding a great many more. Deputy Chief Inspector Calabresi, of the anti-terrorism squad, headed the investigation. Next morning he told the press, 'This is the work of left-wing extremists, there can be absolutely no doubt about it.' Both on the day of the explosion and those following, several anarchist activists were arrested, and one of them, Giuseppe Pinelli, died after falling out of the window of Calabresi's office on the fourth floor of the Questura building where he was being questioned. The police announced that he committed suicide. The far-left organisation Lotta Continua then embarked on an intensive press campaign against Deputy Chief Inspector Calabresi and in defence of the anarchists. In 1971 it was to result in the opening of an investigation into Pinelli's death; the release of the anarchist activist Valpreda, accused of planting the bomb; and the refocusing on the investigation into right-wing extremist circles. In 1972, Luigi Calabresi was assassinated. No one has ever claimed responsibility for his murder, and his assassins have never been identified, or at least not until this morning's arrests, sixteen years after the event and twelve years after the disbanding of the organisation. Watch this space.

Lisa arrives at work very early because she is running the place almost single-handed during the holiday period. This can be oppressive at times. Through the bay windows she spots Cristina making her way towards the clinic, dragging a huge wheelie suitcase. She looks crumpled and tired. A surge of affection and remorse. *We used to be friends, and she has always behaved well towards me. I sent her Filippo. It's wrong of me to hold that wretched novel against her. Bad faith. Besides, I need her, that's probably why I feel this sudden burst of affection.* Cristina pushes open the door and Lisa goes over to greet her with a kiss.

'It's lovely to see you. Did you have a good holiday? Have you come straight from the airport? There was no need to rush.'

'I already delayed my return by two days. I phoned in, but all the same...'

'No problem. Things are quiet at the moment, as you know. I postponed or cancelled your appointments, and I've rescheduled your timetable, it's all on your desk. Everything's fine. Sit down. I'm going to make us an espresso. You look as if you could do with one.'

Cristina sits down in one of the armchairs in the waiting room, her suitcase beside her, her hands folded on her knees. Lisa returns carrying a tray with two plastic cups and a plate of biscuits prettily arranged in the shape of a flower. Cristina stares at the tray with tears in her eyes.

'That's sweet of you...'

Without a word, Lisa sits down beside her and puts her hand on her arm. Cristina looks for a handkerchief and blows her nose.

'Giorgio, my ex, was passing through New York on Monday. My son told me when I got back from my holiday in the Rockies. I wanted to see him again, that's why I delayed my return.'

'And?'

'And it went very badly. Lisa, I live alone in Paris, I feel increasingly isolated, my friends are melting away one by one. Now that I'm no longer the wife of a famous journalist, I feel as if no one's interested in me any more. I'm old and I've had it. He doesn't seem to be suffering from loneliness. She's beautiful, blonde and American, the same age as our son, and she's pregnant.'

Cristina stops, choked. Lisa holds out her cup of coffee.
'Drink, it'll get cold.'

They drink and nibble the biscuits in silence, then Cristina continues: 'And to make everything worse, last night, when I got home, I found that someone had been in my apartment while I was away. I don't think the intruder took anything, but he made sure to leave traces of his presence, a full glass, a book open on a table, little things like that. I was scared, really scared. I spent the night at a hotel near my place, but didn't get a wink of sleep. It's all too much, you know – Giorgio, tiredness, jet lag, this violation … I'm falling apart.'

'Who could have done that? Why? Has anyone already threatened you?'

'I'm convinced it's Filippo.'

'Filippo? Why? Do you have any proof?'

'No. None. A feeling, a hunch, I don't know how to explain it.'

'Why would he do that?'

'I have no idea…'

'What are you going to do? Confront him? Kick him out of the flat?'

'I don't know.'

Lisa picks up the tray.

'I'm going to make some more coffee. We both need it.'

When she comes back with the espressos, she finds that Cristina hasn't budged. Lisa sits down facing her, comfortably ensconcing herself in her armchair.

'This Filippo is a strange character. Ever since his novel came out, I've done my utmost to find out the exact circumstances surrounding Carlo's death. I now have some definite evidence, which I intend to publish very soon. And the facts contained in this evidence don't fit at all with his story. He was never on the run with Carlo, and the sole source for his account of the bank robbery is a newspaper article. Which is not a problem, that's how all novelists work. But he's deliberately working hard to maintain a degree of ambiguity, egged on by his publisher by the way. But by playing on that, he is putting himself in danger. The Italian authorities are going to request his extradition; they're capable of judging him on the basis of what he's written in his book and of pinning the execution of the *carabiniere* and the security guard on him. It is vital that he states, once and for all, and publicly, that his story is a work of fiction and is in no way autobiographical. It's not difficult, but it is urgent. I simply can't understand why he refuses to do so.'

'Have you said all that to him?'

'No. In fact I don't even know him. I've only met him once, and that was when he arrived in France over a year ago. I helped him as best I could, and largely thanks to you, but I don't particularly like him, and I have the feeling that it's mutual. If I suggest we meet, I don't think he'll accept.'

'Yes, you're probably right.'

The two women finish their coffee in silence. Then Cristina says, 'I have an idea. I can phone him and tell him that you'd like to see him. He's bound to be reluctant, so then I'll suggest, if that's OK with you, that I come too, and then maybe he'll agree. When you've told him everything you have to say, you can go and leave me with him. I'll switch the conversation to my little problem with my apartment – it's easier in person than over the phone. I'll see how he reacts.'

'Good plan, OK. When are you going to call him?'

'Later on, at two, when he wakes up. And I'll arrange to meet him this evening, at 7.30, near my place at the Café Pouchkine. We can go there together when we leave here. It's direct on the Métro.'

'Perfect. That suits me. You have two appointments this morning. Do you want me to rearrange them?'

'No, absolutely not! It'll do me good to think about something else.'

She rises. 'And thanks for everything, Lisa.'

Cristina leaves the room pulling her suitcase and goes off

to shut herself in her consulting room. Lisa stares after her, feeling vaguely awkward. *No reason to feel awkward. I'm going to meet him. Perfect. It's what I wanted, isn't it?*

In the course of the morning, the news of the arrest of Sofri, Pietrostefani and Bompressi, charged with murdering Luigi Calabresi, rapidly spreads among the Italian refugees. It is transmitted via phone calls from families and friends, and by the Italian radio stations, which they all rush to tune into. This development sends shock waves through the community. An impromptu meeting is called at the law firm's offices that same evening. Between her two appointments, Lisa drops in to see Cristina in her consulting room at around eleven.

'Can we meet Filippo tomorrow instead of tonight? Are you free?'

Cristina pulls a face.

'On one condition. You come and sleep at my place tonight. I'm scared to go back to my apartment on my own in case I find myself face to face with either Filippo or a stranger, which would be just as bad. And I've had enough of the hotel.'

'OK, we'll figure something out.'

A dozen Italian refugees gather at the law firm's offices, all very shaken. They hadn't spotted any warning signs of this wave of arrests, which at first sight seem utterly baffling. The lawyers give some preliminary information.

'It's not good news. All three are in prison right now.'

Chiara groans. Giovanni nudges her thoughtlessly.

'That'll teach all of you in Lotta Continua. You've preached at us often enough. We've brought everything that has happened down on ourselves. We should never have taken up arms. Maybe now you'll understand how the Italian state operates. And not be so smart.'

Chiara, on the brink of tears, turns away from him and speaks to the lawyers.

'Charged with what, exactly?'

'Sofri and Pietrostefani with being behind the assassination of Luigi Calabresi. Bompressi charged with assassinating him.'

'In 1972! And they haven't woken up till now...'

'That's not all. They are also accused of committing a string of bank robberies since the '70s.'

Lisa murmurs, 'Bank robberies! Well, well. Just like Carlo.'

A male voice, 'It really is nonsense.'

Chiara, who is trying to collect herself, turns to the lawyers, 'Do they have any proof?'

'According to the information we've received, no proof, just the testimony of an informant who turned witness for the state and who claims to have driven the getaway car during the Calabresi operation.'

'His name?'

'Leonardo Marino.'

Three or four people turn round to look at Chiara, who hangs her head.

'OK, OK, I knew him well. We were friends through Lotta Continua. Afterwards, I came to France. I know he joined the Italian Communist Party a few years ago.'

Giovanni, in a mocking tone, 'Friends? Are you kidding? Not only did you lecture us on politics, but on top of that you were never particularly discerning in your choice of lovers.'

'It was a long time ago.'

'All the same. He was already a shit. Shall I refresh your memory?'

They go out into the corridor to continue their quarrel in hushed tones then, when Chiara ends up with tears in her eyes, Giovanni sets about comforting her.

In the lawyers' offices, the heated discussion goes on.

One man who has lived in France for many long years even though he is not the subject of any proceedings in Italy, talks about one of the reasons he departed: 'It's outrageous. What is the Italian justice system about? It's a farce. I remember in

1969, when Calabresi told them that Pinelli had committed suicide by jumping out of his office window, the judges swallowed his story without batting an eyelid. Then, when it was proved that Pinelli hadn't killed himself, the judge didn't back down, he wrote in black and white that it was out of the question that Pinelli could have been assassinated, so he must have suffered from a "sudden indisposition" that made him jump out of the window. It was noted as a death from "accidental causes": the man deserves a prize for his literary inventiveness.'

'Sixteen years after the event, no one's ever been charged. Then without warning, they suddenly arrest Sofri – charismatic leader of a group that has never called on its members to take up arms – for murder. A country of madmen.'

'No, it's not outrageous and they're not mad. They know they're in the midst of a dangerous crisis. If they want to remain in power, the best way is to continue to foment fear of the reds. They are widening the circle of the damned, that's all.'

'And do you think that the spectre of red terrorism from left-wing extremists is enough to guarantee that they'll remain in power? That's according us a great deal of importance.'

'Fear of the reds, when there was a real Communist Party, perhaps. But not of us. We carry no more weight than a feather when set against the behemoth of international communism. No, those shoes are too big to fill. We'll never fill the void left by the decline of the USSR.'

'He's right. It won't work.'

'Not at international level. At the Italian level, they can try putting on an epic performance: we're the baddies who play the leading roles and fill the courts, we make their headlines. And behind the scenes, their own dirty tricks are magicked away: all the fear-mongering, massacres on a huge scale, the secret services, the P2 Lodge, the mafia. After all, Italy's the home of opera. If we ask the judge in the Pinelli case to write the libretto, the show is bound to be convincing.'

Lisa listens without comment, her face drawn, exhausted

by her day at work. No desire to take part in such an abstract discussion. Roberto must be feeling the same way: 'Right, let's stop this global theorising and see whether we can achieve something here on the ground.'

Her words land like a cold shower on all present, who fall silent. Lisa, who has been mulling over the arrests all day to try and assimilate something so seemingly incomprehensible, takes advantage of the lull to speak, despite her fatigue.

'I think that last year's operation involving Carlo was just a trial run. This is the final coup. One question has been haunting me since this morning: why dig up that assassination from 1972 – sixteen long years ago – and why dig it up now? For what it's worth I have a possible answer. The first indiscriminate massacre; ultra-right terrorism; Piazza Fontana, 1969. The first political execution that the far left claimed responsibility for was carried out in 1976 by the Red Brigades. This was seven years after Piazza Fontana and the hundreds of dead in the successive massacres that took place regularly between 1969 and 1976, plus the attempted coup d'état, and all the abuses we know about.

'At the time we believed we were taking up arms not so much out of choice but because we were forced to by our enemies. I'm speaking for the Red Brigades, of course. To pin Calabresi's assassination on Sofri and his friends is to say: terrorism – whether from the far right or the far left – (both took place at around the same time) – is more or less the same thing. Let's reject both and put it all behind us.

'And why strike now? Because the government and our enemies think they can get away with it, that we're beaten, that we're no longer capable of organising a broad enough protest movement to force them to back down. In the way the movement did between 1969 and 1972 over the Piazza Fontana massacre and Pinelli's assassination, when it succeeded in implicating the far right and forcing the judges to release the anarchists. If they're right, we're screwed. But Italian society won't be any better off as a result. The ruling class doesn't know it because they're barbarians, yet a country that represses its history rots from within.'

A silence, then Lisa continues: 'For my part, I've carried on working. I'm seeing Filippo Zuliani tomorrow to keep him informed, and we'll see what he has to say about my findings. Then I'll come and see you.'

Chiara, who has just come back into the room, shouts, 'Give us a break from that guy and the hold-up. An author of airport novels isn't in the same league as a man like Sofri.'

'Those who are in the same league, as you put it, are Carlo and Sofri. Even if you don't like the fact that it puts Sofri on a par with people he's never approved of and vice versa, I've been convinced for a while now that, like it or not it makes no difference, we are all in the same boat. And with these arrests, you and your mates will eventually realise it. Zuliani is a hiccup. An airport novel maybe, but the secret service was still riled enough to get on his case...'

She stops, hears the voice of Pier-Luigi, tinged with irony, *'What do you imagine? That everything said in those meetings remains confidential?'* and tails off mid-sentence, too late perhaps. Giovanni, who has come back into the room on Chiara's heels, leaps to his feet.

'What are you talking about? Do you have information that you're keeping from us?'

'No, nothing special, we'll see later. Let's get back to Sofri and his two friends.'

She turns to the lawyer who sits saying nothing.

'The question remains: what can we do?'

After the meeting, Lisa goes off to find Cristina who has been whiling away the time dozing in a cinema, and they return to Neuilly together. In the lift, Cristina rummages in her bag for ages looking for her keys. Lisa senses her agitation.

'At this hour, Filippo isn't here. You're not likely to bump into him.'

'I know.'

Cristina carries on rummaging, tips the contents of her bag on to the landing scattering things everywhere, but still no keys.

'I'm sorry, Lisa, I'm at the end of my tether. I can't help wondering what I'm going to find when I open my door. When I spoke to Filippo on the telephone earlier, I had the feeling someone was listening in, that there was someone else on the line. It sounded like breathing. I know it makes no sense. I'm hoping things will be better tomorrow. In any case, thanks for your support.'

Lisa picks up the bunch of keys from under a packet of tissues, and holds it out to Cristina. They go through the front door and then the inner door. Cristina switches on the light and glances around anxiously. Everything seems in order. She looks down. On the floor at her feet, a brown manila envelope, immediately recognisable as identical to the one containing the manuscript of *Escape* which Filippo had deposited. Cristina is certain it wasn't there yesterday evening; he must have slipped it under the door. The envelope is as tempting as sin, and gives her a thrill. Whatever happens, Lisa mustn't notice anything. She bends down, picks it up casually and slips it into the outside pocket of her suitcase, then tells Lisa: 'Everything seems to be as it should, in the state I left it last night. Come, I'll show you the bathroom and give you towels and a pair of pyjamas. We're going to sleep in the same bed, if you don't mind. It's at least two metres wide so it should be big enough for two small women like us.'

When Lisa has finished in the bathroom, Cristina locks herself in with her suitcase. She sits down at her dressing table, retrieves the envelope and opens it. Twenty or so manuscript pages, covered in the fine, cramped handwriting she knows well. A hot flush. She skims the first few pages. Mitsouko, the chignon, the wooden hair slides, the dark floor, the glass-and-steel furniture, the white duvet … she chokes, puts the pages down on the table, slips them under her make-up bag, closes her eyes and lets a few seconds go by. She is mystified. Who is this youth who has the cheek to force her to acknowledge that he broke into her apartment and that he wants to pretty much rape her? Reaction number one: kick him out of the studio flat and out of her life immediately. It's the only sensible thing to do. She opens her eyes and looks at herself in the mirror, then meticulously begins to remove her make-up. She examines the lines at the corners of her mouth, the dark rings under her eyes and runs her hand over the skin of her neck, a merciless giveaway of a woman's age. Reaction number two: rape, let's not exaggerate, all very symbolic and literary. Admission: she may find this constant presence on the other side of the wall threatening, but it also excites her, a game of seduction and power. *How can I not admit that I enjoy it? And I like being the woman described in this piece? What if this is a chance to experience love once again? Who am I to refuse it?* Make-up removed, the confusion remains. She has the feeling she has lost her bearings. See what happens when she meets him tomorrow.

29 July, Paris

Another crisis meeting at the publisher's, just before the company closes for two weeks in August.

'After yesterday morning's arrests in Italy, it's clear that the Italian government is launching a full-scale operation against the remnants of the far left. It is an operation that goes way beyond both the book and the person of Filippo Zuliani. This Sofri is not a dangerous lunatic. I believe, no, I'm certain I published something by him in an anthology of articles which was, if not academic, at least reputable. I'd understood that he could be considered as an Italian intellectual and that it was acceptable to associate with him. And the Italian intellectuals with whom we regularly work also considered him as such. I am completely baffled by these arrests. You have to admit that Italian politics are turbulent, often extremely violent, and pretty much unfathomable to an outsider, but that's not the problem.' He turns to Adèle. 'As far as we're concerned, we put a complete block on all media exposure for *Escape*. In any case, at the beginning of August, everything comes to a standstill. Come September, we'll see how the situation has developed in Italy.'

'Understood. I should warn you we've received several phone calls from people wanting Filippo's home address. Of course I've given strict instructions that no such information should be given out. But with the continual stream of hate mail, it's rather worrying.'

The publisher turns to the lawyer.

'Given the new circumstances in which our Italian neighbours now find themselves, is an extradition request likely?'

'It is on the cards. The arrest of Sofri, Pietrostefani and Bompressi is an operation on a different scale from Prosecutor Sebastiani's attack on Zuliani. The book is merely a pretext. I smell trouble.'

'Has our author already been granted asylum? If so, is it temporary or permanent? Does the government intend to renege on its decision?'

'Before giving you a definite answer, I need to find out for certain.'

'Do so, and do it fast. In any case, it would be prudent to remove all traces of our various efforts on behalf of Zuliani, including the lobbying. I'm leaving for the United States this evening. I'll call you tomorrow to let you know where you can get hold of me if necessary.'

Lisa and Cristina leave the offices of La Défense together and seat themselves at a table at the back of the Café Pouchkine to wait for Filippo, who has agreed to meet them at 7.30. The two women sit in silence. Lisa is wondering whether Cristina will be a reliable ally in this conversation, which is bound to be very confrontational, no doubt about that. She is aware of Cristina's uncertainty, but doesn't understand the reason. Must avoid finding herself out on a limb. Don't introduce her into the game.

Filippo stands framed in the doorway, impeccably punctual, his slim form clothed in a beautifully tailored, beige linen suit and a bright-red shirt open at the neck. He glances around the room, spots the two women and makes his way over to their table, a half-smile on his lips. Cristina is certain of only one thing: he is no longer the man who dumped her three months earlier in this very café. Now there is not even the slightest falter in his step or hesitation in his bearing, his style of shaking hands and sitting down, or leaning over his glass as if he didn't know exactly where or who he was. The vague, evasive gaze. All that has gone. An assured manner, visible elegance. Even his features have changed. In what way? Cheeks thinner. And his mouth … Gone the boyish pout. Very well-defined, firm lips. She lets her gaze linger on his mouth.

Having reached their table, Filippo gives a pronounced smile, leans towards Cristina, takes her hand, raises it and brushes it with his lips. He murmurs, 'Mitsouko?' Cristina laughs, she loves the thrill of the chase and seduction, when the game is well played, and she finds it very well played indeed. She suddenly realises how desperately she misses it. 'How did you guess?' she replies, leaving her hand in his a little longer than etiquette dictates. Then she turns to Lisa: 'Should I make the introductions?'

Filippo bows to Lisa with a certain stiffness:

'No need, I believe we already know one another.' He proffers his hand. She takes it after a moment's delay, shakes it and can't help saying: 'I wouldn't have recognised you.'

Filippo sits down opposite her, smiling, relaxed.

'Why? Has life in Paris changed me so much?'

Lisa waits before replying. Yes, he has changed a great deal, and he knows it. He no longer has that helpless look of a lost street kid, and is beginning to look like a successful author, the darling of a major Paris publishing house. This is not going to make her task any easier. Her strategy relied on intimidation and fear. A simple glance at the man facing her, and she knows it won't work. Well, at least I'll have tried, and I'll have told him. Roberto will be satisfied. I'll be able to publish.

Cristina orders cocktails for all of them. Once the drinks have arrived, Filippo leans towards Lisa.

'I've got a date this evening, I don't have much time. Cristina told me you wanted to speak to me. Have you got something to tell me?'

'Are you aware of what's going on in Italy at the moment?'

'Only vaguely. I don't read the Italian papers, but my publisher filled me in.'

'For the last month there's been a relentless and very vitriolic press campaign against your book and against you. At first you were described as a bastard who exploits the misfortune of the victims to make money. And then the campaign was stepped up. The police have produced a witness who claims you were at the scene of the hold-up. Ever since, the press has been having a field day. You've become at least an active witness to the hold-up if not one of the principle killers. The next stage will be for the courts and the Italian government to demand your extradition.'

She stops for a moment.

'You've heard about the arrest of Sofri, Pietrostefani and Bompressi in Italy yesterday?'

'No. And I have no idea who they are.'

'Former political leaders of the far left, like Carlo. It doesn't matter. Their arrest means that the dogs have been unleashed against them and all those of their ilk, so for you it means that the extradition request is imminent. I think the French government will grant it, because your status as a political refugee is very precarious, and won't be upheld. Our lawyers aren't handling your case, remember. Once you're in the hands of the courts, you'll go straight to prison. You'll be tried for your escape, but above all, the courts will make you carry the can for the hold-up in Via Del Battifolle. It won't be hard given their surprise witness and your wonderful novel, which describes the chain of events so vividly, just as if you had experienced them at first-hand. Wrong as it may seem, your novel will be interpreted as an admission of your involvement in the robbery. You were able to portray it so well because you were there. And we both know that you have no alibi. In the current political climate, you're likely to get at least twenty years inside. Are you aware of all that?'

'Yes, more or less. I know that my fellow Italians see me as an accomplice.'

'You don't seem too bothered by it.'

'No, I'm not. And you've spoken at length, but I still don't understand why you care what happens to me, nor what it is you want to say to me.'

'I don't care what happens to you, but I do care what happens to us. Carlo belonged to a political movement, and so did I. Anything that affects him, affects us all. If Carlo goes down in history as a gangster who robbed banks to live the high life with his criminal gang, whether in Rome or Milan, we all pay the political price. And that's a very high price to pay.'

'You know very well that I'm not interested in your lessons in politics.'

'I know. But that doesn't mean that politics isn't interested in you. So let me finish. Seeing as I was affected by Carlo's death, I investigated what really happened. I now know the identity of the miracle witness who claims to have seen you in the Via Del Battifolle. He's a stooge of the neo-fascists and the secret service. He knew Carlo from jail. He's the one who organised your escape and the fatal sting outside the Milan bank. I'm going to make sure that the French press knows about it and publishes the story.'

'Fine, that's what you think, and of course you're free to do what you want. But again, what has it got to do with me?'

'I'd like you to state publicly that your book is a novel, a story you invented based on newspaper articles, and that you were never on the run with Carlo. In other words, I'd like you to tell what we both know to be the truth and say that the book is a pure work of fiction. Doing so will have the dual advantage of putting you out of danger since no one's going to extradite a novelist. And it will help us to rehabilitate Carlo.'

'Rehabilitate Carlo! You really don't get it, do you?'

Filippo turns to Cristina, places his hand on the table very close to hers, and addresses her. These words are for her:

'I loved Carlo. I listened to him for hours on end. He would talk about his battles, describe the colour of violence, the thrill of combat to the death. He fascinated me. He gave a meaning to my own rebellion, which I'd never been able to articulate. And above all, he taught me to love weighty words, words laden with matter, energy, emotion, words that now enable me to live. When we escaped, when we found ourselves in the rubbish skip, when I was drowning, he held his hand out to me, his touch saved me from my own panic, forever. Then I knew that I could die for him, for nothing, with pleasure. When he was killed, I wrote *Escape* out of loyalty and out of love.' He turns to Lisa: 'And you're asking me to deny all that, his life and mine, to protect myself and for the sake of your abstract ideas? For your outdated memories of a man who's been dead for ages? Don't count on me. Not today, not ever.'

Then he gets up, turns his back on the two women and walks out. Cristina rushes after him, without a word. Lisa, dumbfounded, rooted to the spot, swallows her defeat.

Cristina catches up with Filippo at the door. She halts him by putting her hand on his arm.

'When I came into the Café Pouchkine, I didn't know what to expect or what might happen afterwards...'

He smiles.

'Now you know. You have a date with me. I'm inviting you

to dinner. I've booked a table at Sébillon, and it's not far from here.'

'What about your job...?'

'I'm not a night watchman any more.'

'That job wasn't worthy of you.'

He slips his arm under hers and guides her. They walk away from the café, he can feel her hip against his, their steps attuned.

'This is the most wonderful evening of my short life.'

Still sitting at the table, Lisa watches them walk off down the sunny street. *Impressive diatribe, impressive exit. I knew I wouldn't get anything out of him. But Roberto won't be able to say anything now. The most puzzling thing is Cristina's extraordinary behaviour. Are women as unreliable as men? Hard to admit. They left without paying. Of course. A pity to spoil such a magnificent exit with such a vulgar detail.*

Lisa bitterly pays for the three cocktails that no one had the time to drink, picks up her belongings and leaves the Café Pouchkine. She can see the couple a hundred metres away, walking off down the street still bathed in sunlight. Almost the same height, they walk at a regular pace, chatting, leaning in towards each other. Cristina occasionally rests her head on Filippo's shoulder. Lisa comments to herself that he is walking on the outside, as recommended in the etiquette guides from the 1900s, to protect his companion from being splashed by vehicles passing at speed, and the stupid thought distracts her.

Just then, a man bumps into her as he rushes out of the porch of an apartment building. She is knocked off balance, protests aloud. The man does not turn round but runs faster. He is wearing a white T-shirt and jeans and a stylish panama hat pulled down over his eyes. Lisa doesn't get a look at his face. Then one thing follows another, as with a well-oiled machine. The man in the panama is closing in on the couple. A motorbike rides slowly up the street, and passes Lisa. The man in the panama catches up with the couple. Lisa hears a gunshot. No mistaking it, she's heard enough in her life to know. A single shot. She freezes, and at the same time sees Filippo collapse, the bike pass the couple in slow motion, the man in the panama jump on to the pillion, the bike roar off, and Cristina spin round and crumple on to the pavement. Lisa springs into action, races towards the two bodies on the ground, screaming, 'Help … Help!'

When she reaches them, she glances at Filippo's body lying face down, a black hole in the centre of his back, his lovely beige jacket scorched. A pool of blood is spreading over the pavement close to his left shoulder. Dead. Too late to do anything. She quickly turns to Cristina, lying on her back, her entire body rigid, her face ashen, the whites of her eyes showing, her jaw locked. Lisa tries to raise Cristina's head, but is unable to. Suddenly her body goes into spasm, shudders, her teeth chattering. Lisa, desperate, doesn't know what to do. She looks up. A few people appear at their windows, alerted by the gunshot and her screams. A stranger is standing next to her.

'I'm a doctor. My surgery is in the apartment building over the road. I heard the shot, and then your screams. This woman is having an epileptic fit. Do you know if it's happened before?'

'No, not that I'm aware of.'

'I've already called an ambulance and the police. You don't look too good either. I'm going to get a chair so you can sit down until the police get here. Don't take it as an excuse to faint, please.'

The ambulance arrives very quickly and Cristina, still unconscious, is driven off to the nearest hospital. Shortly afterwards, three police cars pull up, sirens wailing. The police block off the street and cordon off the crime scene. A plain-clothes police officer takes Lisa to one side and starts questioning her, while others try and gather statements from the neighbours.

For the time being, Lisa is the only witness. ID? Italian refugee. Aha … Did she know the victim? Yes, Filippo Zuliani, also an Italian. The police officer looks up from his notebook.

'The guy who wrote a book about how he assassinated a *carabiniere*, and boasts about it?'

Lisa shrugs helplessly.

'If you like…'

The police officer barely lowers his voice.

'Good riddance.'

Then she has to say, and repeat over again, the same words, explain what the three of them had been doing at the Café Pouchkine, the couple leaving together first, Lisa staying behind to pay. No, they hadn't had a quarrel.

'That's not what the barman says.'

It was a discussion, they had disagreed, but it wasn't a quarrel. She had not fallen out with the dead man. Well … not like that. When she came out, the man in the panama, no, she hadn't seen his face. Height, build, age … in his thirties or forties, not all that young, quite well-built, that was all she could say. The motorbike, no, she hadn't seen the licence plate, not even certain whether it had one … the police officer presses her … or not.

When he repeats his questions for the fourth time, night has fallen and Lisa, exhausted, asks him what he's driving at, exactly.

'All three of you are Italian, two of you are refugees with a dodgy background, possible disagreements between you back in Italy, where there are lots of shootings. You met at the café, there was a heated discussion, you didn't leave with him. You saw the killers, but you haven't given me any useful information. So I'm asking myself, and I'm asking you: did you lure this Filippo into a trap and give the signal to the killers?'

Probably due to the shock of the murder or the exhaustion of being interrogated, Lisa bursts out laughing.

'I think you're as paranoid as I am. But you've got a point. I'm not able to prove that I didn't kill Filippo Zuliani.'

Now she understands what the officer wants to get out of her, she is able to breathe more easily. She is no longer in the surreal realm of the nightmare. She gets her breath back, finds her nerve, and casts her eye over the crime scene. The body has been removed, the job of the police seems to be done. A small group of onlookers is still hanging around, Roberto is in the front row. How did he hear? Always there when she needs him. The sight of him comforts her, she waves to him, smiles at him.

Shortly afterwards the police pack up their equipment. Lisa, whose home and workplace addresses have been checked out, is allowed to go home – she'll be summoned to the police station later. She falls into Roberto's arms. The worst of the shock has been cushioned. Too late to cry. A pity.

Her staunch friend has thought of everything. Nothing like a good meal to help face up to death. In their infinite wisdom, both French and Italian traditions prescribe a feast after a funeral. Even more reason for one after an assassination. So he takes her for dinner to the best local eatery, the only one that stays open so late. Sébillon, famed for its leg of lamb.

Lisa has great difficulty regaining her composure. She is caught up in the brutality of the absurd, torn between hysteria and despair. As they sit down at their table, Roberto first of all asks after Cristina.

'You told me she was coming to the Café Pouchkine with you. I looked everywhere for her, but I couldn't find her.'

'After our meeting, she left with Filippo, to take him home to bed.'

'So he came off best in your duel?'

'I think that now I can admit it, yes, definitely. I didn't even get off the ground and he was flying in the stratosphere. So, Cristina was on Filippo's arm when he was shot.'

'Shit!'

'She had an epileptic fit and was taken to hospital, I don't know which one. And right now, I don't care. I'll think about it tomorrow.'

She sips a pleasant Loire wine, breathes deeply then takes the plunge.

'Roberto, I'd never have thought our secret service would assassinate Filippo. I'm thinking it's more likely to be Bonamico.'

'Stop fantasising, please. Not now. It's creepy. And eat.'

'Why did they kill him? Because they knew we were on Bonamico's trail, and that we have proof? I don't see the connection.'

'That's absurd. They didn't know. Who could have told them? Neither you nor I, and no one else knows about your investigation. Satisfied?'

Lisa attacks her food. Delicious lamb, cooked to perfection, the meat melts in her mouth. It's tricky, cooking leg of lamb. Someone knew. She thought of her telephone conversations with Stefania, the *Corriere di Brescia* journalist. *'My boss asked me if I was in contact with you.'* The information had surfaced and quickly. Am I the one who sparked the whole thing off? No way I can tell Roberto. Stefania's voice continues to ring in her ears.

Suddenly she freezes, fork halfway to her mouth. What had Stefania said? Bonamico, the lover of the Tomasino girl, the Brescia banking family, a photo from 1974, a terrifying face, the eyebrows joined, the scar ... Just like Marco in *Escape*: eyebrows, scar, vicious, brutal ... Filippo saw Bonamico with Carlo, he says so in his book. And the moment Prosecutor Sebastiani tried to bring him back to Italy to stand trial – and was likely to succeed – was the moment Filippo was sentenced to death. Lisa closes her eyes. A hollow ache in her chest. Hard to accept. Even the story he told me about his and Carlo's escape, more than a year ago, was no more reliable than the rest. At the end of the day, maybe he did take part in the hold-up after all. I'll never know. No choice, I'll have to live with it. She slowly readjusts to the reality of the restaurant, Roberto, their conversation. It's no longer a time for passion, but for appraisal.

In a neutral voice, she says, 'The French police will conduct a lengthy investigation into Filippo's assassination, but they won't find the killers. They'll only be sure of one thing. The *modus operandi*: a professional hit man, a single bullet shot at point-blank range, an accomplice on a motorbike, speedy getaway, no clues, no witnesses, it's a professional hit. Then a police officer will recall having read Filippo's book: Carlo's double was shot after the Rome gang informed on him. To avenge him, Filippo's double shoots Marco, the leader of the Rome gang, who take their revenge by having Filippo killed. It all makes sense.'

'You're talking nonsense.'

'You'll see. I'm willing to bet on it.'

Roberto desperately casts about for a topic of conversation to distract her.

'It would be better to talk about our own affairs. There's no reason not to continue with Bonamico. Who shall we contact to publish your report?'

Lisa stops eating, she looks straight through Roberto, and stares into the far distance.

'I don't think you realise what's just happened. We're not going to publish anything at all. There's no point. There's nothing more to be done. Nobody can fight against a death as romantic as Filippo's. He's become a sort of legend, that of the hoodlum at a turning point in his life – he steals, he kills, he writes and he dies at the age of twenty-three, shot on the streets of Paris by strangers, with a bullet straight through his heart. Twenty-three years old, just think. The age I was when I met Carlo. Filippo is a comet, and his book will now be sacrosanct. He has taken Carlo off into a world of his own. Nothing more to be done. Adieu, Carlo, *bon voyage.*'

'Are you giving up?'

Still gazing into the distance, she says nothing for a while.

'Yes, I'm giving up. That particular battle's lost. If I want to try and salvage our past, there's only one thing left for me to do. Write novels.'

AFTERWORD

Dominique Manotti uses two historical references that may be unfamiliar to readers, the more so since the second is fictitious. Years of Lead and Years of Fire frame the events of *Escape*. Its author is a former trade unionist and political militant, for many years a professor of nineteenth-century history at the University of Vincennes during its most actively radical period. Manotti's ten novels all explore unholy alliances forged between crime and politics. *Escape* is no different but changes context – from Poland to Korea to Turkey in previous works – and looks south to Italy during the years of Red Brigades activism in the 1970s and '80s.

Escape's origins are steeped in the 'Republic of Salò', named after the town near Brescia where Mussolini sought to establish his Republican Fascist Party as his army was forced northwards from Rome. It became known as the Repubblica Sociale Italiana, lasting from 1943 to 1945, as a client state of German Nazism, doomed to destruction by the Allies and partisans. Echoes of its politics reverberated down the generations: through the fascist Ordine Nuovo waging a clandestine terror campaign to Alessandra Mussolini's recent People of Freedom, a revival of her grandfather's questionable legacy. As Manotti has written elsewhere: 'To understand Italy, one has to remember the immense and profound support for Mussolini and the proximity of the War to the events in this book. Fascism had only been defeated for twenty-five years in 1968, leaving numerous live fascist cells behind.'

Years of Lead describes a period of political turmoil and

flying bullets in Italy, sparked by the 1969 Piazza Fontana bombing in Milan that killed seventeen and wounded ninety people. It was followed by probably dozens of undisclosed acts of terrorism, including the 1970 bomb that killed six in the southern Gioia Tauro train station; the 1972 car bombing that killed three police officers in Pateano, northern Italy; the 1974 *Italicus* train bombing that killed twelve in the Apennines between Florence and Bologna; the 1974 massacre in Brescia's Piazza della Loggia that killed eight anti-fascist protesters and wounded 100; the 1980 plane crash near the Sicilian island of Ustica, the 1980 Bologna train station bombing that killed eighty-five and wounded over 200; and the 1984 Rapido 904 massacre in which sixteen died when a bomb exploded on the Florence-Bologna train line. It was only in April 2014 that Prime Minister Matteo Renzi declassified secret files on a minority of the most notorious cases, confirming the involvement of the neo-fascist Ordine Nuovo and, latterly, of its offshoot the Armed Revolutionary Nucleo (ARN). Terrorism, involving the indiscriminate murder of civilians, was routinely used by the Right in order to blame and discredit the Left, and to foment mass insecurity and unrest. Is *Escape*, written two years before the disclosures, a case of fiction anticipating political disclosure of historical fact?

The Years of Fire is a term invented by the book's first protagonist Carlo, a Red Brigades leader. His strategy is to counter the deadening nature of the Years of Lead via propaganda through targeted assassinations and popular insurrection, destined to catch fire and burn brightly. Revealed are the lengths to which the state will go to create a 'strategy of tension' to sow disorder, resulting in popular demand for imposed order. In 1969, political parties across the spectrum from neo-fascist to centre-left were panicked at the imminent prospect of the majority Italian Communist Party winning elections with 36 per cent of the votes. No left-wing party was ever allowed to come that close to power again.

At a recent conference (at City University, London, in May 2014), Manotti was asked why she had turned from political activism to writing crime novels. She replied, *'par désespoir.'* She could as well have quoted herself, speaking as Carlo's comrade, Lisa, at the close of this stranger-than-fiction history: 'That particular battle's lost. If I want to try and salvage our past, there's only one thing left for me to do. Write novels.'

Amanda Hopkinson
May 2014